How To Stick A Dart In Your Head

By Eric J. Hill

EJHProductions
121 Deer Hollow Road
Poughquag, NY 12570

Dedication and Acknowledgement

This book is dedicated to my parents, John and Marilyn Hill, because they trusted me when I was a boy and left me to my own devices, literally, way too often. Their non-supervision made it possible for me to get into a lot of the situations described in this book in the first place. But if I told you that all of the scenes in this book really happened, except for the parts I made up, you probably wouldn't believe me, so I won't tell you that. This book is entirely a work of fiction, and any resemblances to any persons, places, animals or things, currently on earth or no longer with us, is totally coincidental. Also, in spite of what you will read in this book, I hope you will continue to treat me as an intelligent and reasonably competent adult, rather than someone who spent most of his younger years creating havoc and chaos every chance he got. Or, maybe you could just *pretend* to treat me that way. I think that would be a nice compromise for both of us.

In contrast to all of the other authors of all the other books I have read in my life, I would like to acknowledge the help and support of hardly anyone since I steadfastly refused to accept advice or help during the writing process. However, regardless of that general attitude on my part, special thanks must go out to my friends, my family, and all of the boys of St. Bernard's School who patiently listened to early versions of the manuscript whether they wanted to or not. Extra special thanks go to Ethan Hendricks who read parts of the first draft and encouraged me to keep writing. Double extra special thanks go to Jack Ungar for being a shining inspiration in my life and for agreeing to be the boy on the cover. So I guess I will admit that I accepted some encouragement and a small bit of advice, but *definitely* not any help. In fact, I got huffy and defensive when any changes or improvements were suggested, particularly when these observations were accurate. This is exactly the kind of thinking that got me into the situations described in these chapters in the first place. My philosophy has always been: "What I don't know will most likely hurt me." Kind of like when you stick a dart in your head. EH

Table of Contents

Chapter 1

Einstein In Reverse

S O I STUCK A DART in my head when I was about twelve years old. It wasn't an easy thing to do, because I only had a hockey stick and a ping-pong table to work with, but somehow I managed it. If nothing else, I was clever and resourceful during those early years.

I stuck an arrow in the toe of my sneaker right around this same time too, but that was a piece of cake. All I had to do was shoot the arrow straight up into the air, wait for it to come back down, and then see how close it would land. It was a simple-minded pastime that I called The Arrow Game. Simple-minded. Classic. Not smart. But at least I wore a football helmet to protect myself when I played it. At times I amazed myself with how really clever I could be.

But the Dart-In-The-Head Story always gets everyone's attention. Like all of my other potentially self destructive escapades it proved that I was gifted in a backwards sort of way. I had talents that were the complete and total opposite of what my mom and dad thought I had. I was like Einstein In Reverse. There was pretty much nothing that I couldn't turn into a near disaster. And along with being resourceful and clever, I had a wide variety of interests too. Looking back at it all now, it's hard to believe how truly clueless I was.

Like, when I broke the window of our kitchen door with a hammer trying to get ice off of it in January. Yes, a hammer. Or, when I almost set our garage on fire experimenting with gasoline and matches. That was a close one, especially since the garage was attached to our house. Or, when I crashed my bike at full speed into my dad's car which was parked in our own driveway. I swear I didn't see it there. Or, when a friend and I set the big hay field behind our house on fire in the middle of the worst drought in decades playing with matches, yet again. Who knew that extended droughts could make things so *dry*? Or, when I blew up a gallon of rubber cement in our charcoal grill because, "I wanted to see what would happen." I'll explain that one later. Or, that time I came home from a Viking Raid with a dead rabbit I'd found on the road and hung it up in my bedroom closet for four months. I had no idea that one little dead rabbit could smell *so* bad. I went through a major Viking Phase during those early years. In fact I still get the urge to attack unsuspecting coastal villages from time to time.

But no one knew about any of this except me. Thank goodness my parents never found out. They would have felt terrible. They thought I was smart, obedient, and overflowing with common sense and practical logic. They trusted me to be home alone, *a lot*. This proved to be a major flaw in their parental supervision system. I got home from school every week day a couple of hours ahead of when they got home from work which gave me plenty of time for boyishly charming witless experimentation. But if you think about it in a certain way, by withholding the truth about all the crazy things I did, I wasn't really *lying* to my parents, I was *protecting* them from the pain of parental disappointment. You have to be nice to your parents. They try so hard to raise you right.

I mean, who wants to be the parents of a boy who sticks darts in his head? Or, a boy who crashes his bike at full speed into parked cars in broad daylight? Or, a boy who blows up a gallon of rubber cement in the backyard grill? Or, a boy who nearly sets fire to the garage? And the garage was attached to the house as I mentioned before. Or, a boy who puts dead rabbits in his bedroom closet? And then, how do you share that kind of information with the parents of normal children?

Imagine, for a moment, my parents are at a cocktail party, chatting casually with the parents of

Mergatroid, The Very Bright And Annoyingly Normal Child.

My Parents, Casually,

"So, how's Mergatroid doing these days?"

The Parents of Mergatroid, The Very Bright And Annoyingly Normal Child, Proudly,

"*Our* little Mergatroid? He's doing just great! Straight A's in school. Captain of his Junior Olympics Curling Squad. Doing really well on the Lithuanian Fluglehorn. Thinking about a career in Reconstructive Nasal Surgery, heading off to Space Camp this summer. What's Eric up to these days?"

My Parents, Evasively,

"*Our* Eric? Oh... ummm... you know... ummm... just the usual. Setting fire to the garage. Crashing into parked cars on his bike. Sticking darts in his head..."

Parents of Mergatroid, Stunned,

"What?"

Chapter 2

It Wasn't Really My Fault

I T WASN'T REALLY MY FAULT that all these things happened to me. I have always felt that my parents were to blame for not providing me with at least a couple of siblings to protect me from myself. I was raised as an only child even though that wasn't true. I had a half-sister who was fifteen years older than me, but she lived in Ohio, so for practical purposes I was on my own. Siblings would have made such a difference in my life. Being an only child puts you at a huge disadvantage. An older, intolerant, repressive sibling would have been very helpful during my formative years, but my parents totally failed me on that one. An older, intolerant, repressive sibling would have taken charge of these potentially dangerous situations. He or she would have wisely questioned my actions, and then whacked me on the head for good measure. Take the "Ice On The

Window Of The Kitchen Door" episode, just for an example.

Me,

"Gosh Sis!, I tried to knock some ice off of the window of the kitchen door with Dad's hammer, and believe it or not, the whole window shattered and fell out onto the patio! Boy, oh boy, was I ever surprised!"

My Hypothetical Older Intolerant Repressive Sibling,

"Wait a minute... did you say Dad's *hammer*?! You used Dad's *hammer* to knock some of the ice off the window of the kitchen door?! You *idiot!" Whack!*

Me,

"Ow!"

See how helpful that would have been? On the other hand, a younger, intolerant, revengeful sibling would have been helpful too, because he or she would have *told* on me. This would have forced my parents to become aware of my total lack of common sense, and they in turn would have taken the necessary steps to keep me under closer surveillance. But I didn't have that kind of support either. Take for example, the near total engulfing of the garage in flames from the "Gasoline And Matches" episode. And don't forget that the garage was attached to the house.

Me,

"Golly, Little Brother, guess what? I poured gasoline on the garage floor and lit it with a match, and guess *what*? I almost set fire to the whole garage! I was *so* surprised! Don't tell Mom and Dad, Ok?"

My Hypothetical Younger Revengeful Sibling,

"Wait a second, did you just say that you poured *gasoline* on the garage floor and lit it with a match? And you were *surprised* that you almost set fire to the garage!? Do you know that it's *attached* to the house? I'm *telling*! Mom! Dad! Eric poured gasoline on the garage floor and lit it with a match!"

My Parents, Surprised, Then Outraged,

"Did you say he poured *gasoline* on the garage floor and lit it with a match!!!? He almost set fire to the garage!? *Our* garage? The one that's *attached* to the house?!! *Eric!!!*"

Me,

"Uh oh."

See how helpful that also would have been? That's pretty much what I saw the other kids in my neighborhood doing to their siblings. I grew up near several families with multiple kids, and as far as I could tell they spent most of their free time hitting each other with blunt objects and ratting each other out to their parents. It seemed as if one of them was always wearing a cast, or hobbling around on crutches, due to some out of control inter-sibling craziness. And believe me, good old fashioned wooden crutches and plaster arm casts made handy blunt objects. From my point of view it was an endless cycle of sibling aggression, blunt objects, crutches, and casts. I also learned that they loved each other very much too. They could happily try to hit each other all day long, but if you dared so much as to *touch* one of them, they all turned on you like a pack of wild dogs. They chased you like a pack of wild dogs too. Thank goodness I was fast.

But there were no siblings for me, no pack that I belonged to. I was flying solo. No Robin to my Batman. No R2D2 to my Luke Skywalker. All I had was me, and I was definitely not a good choice of companion for me to be hanging out with. With me it was all trial and error, but mostly it was error. I had no one to advise me, or to tell on me, and I certainly wasn't going to tell on myself. That would've been *really* dumb.

So, to stay with our earlier example, I didn't *mean* to break the window of the kitchen door by trying to knock the ice off of it with a hammer. It seemed to make sense to my way of thinking. There was ice on the window of the kitchen door. I wanted to be helpful and remove it. My intentions were good. I just made a bad choice of tools. I went into the garage and thoughtfully selected a mid-sized hammer from my dad's tool bench to do the job. I went back around to the kitchen door and gave the ice a light rap with the hammer. Nothing happened. I gave it a much heartier whack with the hammer. A whole lot happened. I mean, the hammer certainly broke the ice, but when it broke the entire window in half, which then fell out and shattered all over the patio steps, I was the most surprised boy in the world. I told my dad that the window had been smashed by a *bird,* like some kind of Mutant Attack Chickadee, or something along those lines.

Chapter 3

Warning! Keep Out Of The Reach Of Only Children

LMOST SETTING THE GARAGE ON fire, an *attached* garage as I keep pointing out, was another example of my inability to foresee cause and effect. It was a rainy day. I was tired of being cooped up down in the playroom on yet another Viking Raid, stabbing Stubbornly Resistant Villagers, aka the couch cushions, with my sword. I always kept a sword handy in those days, and a shield and spear too. You'd think those Villagers would have learned to just give up, but they always came back for more. They were Stubborn, those Villagers, and *really* Resistant.

I finally got pretty tired of stabbing Stubborn Resistant Villagers, so I decided to go out into the garage and find something different to do. I decided to do something really dumb, and I *don't* recommend it. I took my dad's can of lawn mower gasoline and began to pour little puddles of gas on the garage floor and then lit the puddles with a match. The first one I lit was a bit disappointing. Not much happened. So I poured out a slightly bigger puddle. It definitely burned higher, but it was nothing special. On the third one I kind of lost control of the can, spilling more than I intended to, but I lit it anyway. That wasn't so smart because a whole lot happened, and it happened really fast. I stood there in total shock as the flames shot up higher and higher until they reached up and licked the garage rafters for a few heart stopping seconds before dying down again. I definitely don't recommend it, especially since the garage was attached to the house. I still get sick thinking about it. Forty years later, when my mom moved out of that house, I went into the garage, and the burnt marks left by the flames on the rafters were still there, grim reminders of my misguided youth.

Let's keep in mind we're talking about the same boy, me, who found an entire gallon of rubber cement on a shelf in the garage one day and decided to try a similar experiment with it, but this time out of doors, thank goodness. The first words I saw printed on the can of rubber cement were *"Flammable"*, and *"Volatile"*. I knew what *"Flammable"* meant, but I wasn't really clear on what *"Volatile"* meant. Now I know.

Out into the backyard I went with my new-found gallon of rubber cement and my ever present book of matches. It was a beautiful sunny afternoon in the heartland of Suburbia, and it was great to be young, alive, and clueless. I opened the can and started making long curly lines with the rubber cement on the back walkway. There was a handy little brush attached to the underside of the large screw-on cap which I assumed was put there for just this sort of thing. I made a nice floral curly design, about three feet long, put a match to one end, and watched it burn. The whole floral curly design burned like a fuse, just like in all those Western Movies I'd seen where they would blow stuff up with sticks of dynamite. For a little while the whole design flamed away dramatically, and then it died out. This had potential.

From curly floral designs I moved on to small landscapes which were really quite nice once they began flaming. Then I did the entire alphabet, in *cursive,* because as everyone knows, good handwriting is important. That was nice. But then I looked at the walkway and realized it now had burnt blackened stuff all over it. Not good. So I got a stiff broom out of the garage and managed to remove most of the evidence from the walkway. But I was still intrigued by the possibilities the can of rubber cement offered, and my mom wouldn't be home for at least a couple of hours.

My next brilliant move was to try out a few new things in our outdoor charcoal grill. I figured, who would care about some more burnt blackened stuff in the charcoal grill? That's what charcoal grills are for, right? I poured a tiny little puddle of the rubber cement into the grill, lit it with a match, and watched it burn. It was nice, but not really interesting. So then I poured a bigger puddle of rubber cement into the grill and lit it. The flames rose about three feet in the air. It was a little scary, but nothing I couldn't handle. I mean, it wasn't even *close* to how scared I got in the garage that day with the gasoline. Plus, the grill was out in the middle of the back yard where I really couldn't do any serious harm, sort of.

I decided that it might be interesting to carefully place the whole gallon sized can of rubber cement into the pool of flames with the cap screwed on as tightly as possible to see what would happen. Nothing happened, at least nothing happened right away. During those moments when nothing was happening, I heard the phone ringing in the house. This was in 1964 when telephones actually made a series of loud *ringing* sounds. My mom called me at home from work every afternoon to see how I was doing. As I mentioned earlier, I always got home from school before either of my parents. It was a flawed system as I had proven many times. The phone rang again. I remember thinking to myself,

"I should really get that can of rubber cement out of those flames..."

But I didn't have time to do so, and please remember there weren't even Answering Machines in those primitive days of telecommunications, so I really had to answer the phone. I left the tightly sealed gallon sized can of rubber cement roasting in the pool of flames on the grill, and ran back up into the house to answer the phone because I knew it was my mom, right on schedule.

Me, Casually Cheerful,
"Hi Mom!"

I always used an optimistic and boyishly charming tone with her. I still do.

My Mom,
"Is everything ok?"

She asked me that every day. She still does.

Me, Even More Cheerfully,
"Yep! Just playing in the back yard!"

I always said that. No point in getting her upset. I mean what was I supposed to say...?

"Just blowing up a gallon of rubber cement in the charcoal grill in the backyard!"

I don't think so.

Me Again, *Very* Cheerfully,
"Just playing in the back yard!"

Repetition is soothing to adults as you probably already know.

As the word, "*yard*", came out of my mouth, the entire gallon can of rubber cement exploded. I mean *really* exploded. I heard a deep, *"Ka-Whumph!"*, followed by a flash of intense bright light that reflected like sudden sunlight in the glass window of the kitchen door. Yes, the same one I had shattered with the hammer that time. The rest of the phone call took about two seconds.

My Mom, Slightly Alarmed,
"What was that *noise*?!"

Me, Desperately Calm,
"*Noise*? You heard a *noise*? Oh... I think maybe a truck backfired out in the road or something..."

My Mom, Relieved,
"Oh, ok, see you in a while."

Me, *Insanely* Calm,
"OK... See you soon..."

Bam! I slammed the phone down, raced out into the backyard, and stopped dead in my tracks at the sight that greeted me. It was like a scene from a war movie. Blobs of flaming rubber cement were spinning through the air like Napalm. Clouds of smoke were wafting across the entire back yard, and little flames were blossoming in a big circle all around the charcoal grill. I ran around the back yard stomping on the flames until they were all out. When I finally extinguished them all, I stood back to see how things looked, and things did not look good at all. In fact things looked really, really bad.

There were at least two dozen little round burnt patches about two or three inches in diameter scattered across the formerly lush green lawn of the back yard. The can of rubber cement was lying about ten feet from the charcoal grill, ripped in half by the explosion with wisps of smokey vapor still hovering over it. But I didn't panic. I knew I still had about two hours to work with before my mom came home. I went and got one of my dad's long handled shovels out of the garage. I carried the ripped open rubber cement can out past the stone wall that bordered the back yard and buried it in the field behind the house. Then I lifted the congealed blob of charcoal and rubber cement out of the grill with the shovel and buried it in the field too. I poured some new charcoal into the grill. It looked pretty good.

Then I got out the lawn mower, set the deck really low, and mowed the entire back lawn really short. This eliminated a lot of the burnt grassy patches, but it still looked dicey. So I went into the house, got a pair of scissors, and for about an hour or so I crawled around in the back yard trimming the burnt patches down so there was no more burned or blackened grass. I gathered up all the little burnt grass clippings and threw them over the stone wall. The problem now was that my handiwork with the scissors had created about twenty strange looking hollowed out little patches of semi-bare earth all over one side of the formerly nice green grassy back lawn. But at least all the burnt parts were gone. I did some rapid calculations and felt pretty secure. I figured it would be dark before my dad got home which was in my favor. My mom never really paid much attention to the lawn. Then I knew my dad would leave early in the morning for his train, so with a little luck he wouldn't see the back yard until the weekend which was a few days away. I was pretty sure I had gotten out of this one, but I went to bed early just to be safe. I will never forget the conversation my parents had that following Saturday morning.

My Dad, Responsibly Puzzled,
 "There's something wrong with the back lawn."

My Mom, Helpfully,
 "What seems to be the problem?"

My Dear Kind-Hearted Dad, More Puzzled,
 "Well, it looks like it has some kind of fungus or lack of fertilizer, or something. There are little bare patches all around on the side of the lawn near the grill."

My Mom, The Lawn Care Expert,
 "Oh, it probably needs fertilizer or lawn food."

My Dad, Agreeably Relieved,

"Yeah, I guess you're right. I'll get some lawn food this weekend."

Me,

I didn't say a word.

So my dad went to the hardware store and got some lawn food or whatever and fussed around with the lawn for a few weeks until it came back to its original condition. Like I said, I never said a word. There was no one to tell on me, and it wasn't really my fault, if you look at it in a certain way.

Chapter 4

It's All Fun And Games Until Someone Sticks A Dart In His Head

S O, AS I STARTED TO say, I stuck a dart in my head during this period of unsupervised boyish self discovery. The rubber cement episode greatly reduced my interest in flammable materials although I must say the lawn looked amazing for several years thereafter. Our downstairs playroom was my main theater of operations on the days when I was home on my own. It was spacious and private, and honestly my room never smelled quite the same after the dead rabbit incident. The playroom ceiling was covered with those 1960's style soft acoustical tiles that supposedly absorbed the loud noises and disturbing sounds that boys seem to make all of the time.

I had some really nice early mornings all by myself downstairs in the playroom watching my black and white TV while crisping up Viking Toast on our electric space heater which, of course, was not supposed to be used for that sort of thing. I used to pretend it was a Viking Campfire and sit by it while guarding my imaginary Viking Warship. I'd tip it over so its back panel was on the floor and then push the bottom of it against the wall. This de-activated the safety device on the underside of the heater which was supposed to prevent it from working when it wasn't fully upright. As I may have mentioned earlier, I was pretty clever at times. So I would have my little electric Viking Campfire all my own right there in the playroom. I would wrap my blanket around my shoulders like a Viking Warrior Guy, lay some slices of bread on the space heater's stainless steel grill, and enjoy my Viking Campfire Toast. Somehow my parents never caught on to this situation as if it were totally normal for the playroom to smell like toast at 6:30 in the morning. They never asked me about the butter and jam stains in the carpet either.

The classic 1960's style acoustical ceiling tiles had thousands of tiny little holes in them that supposedly absorbed the bellowing of Viking War Cries, the desperate yells of Stubborn Resistant Villagers, and other loud noises associated with the sacking of unsuspecting coastal villages. The tiles themselves were made from a mysterious soft material, and probably had Asbestos in them, but nobody cared back then. It was an innocent time. I mean our family would gather together in the living room each week to watch The Flintstones on Prime Time TV. *The Flintstones.* Fred, Barney, Betty, Bam-Bam, and of course, "*Wilma...!!!*" I'm serious.

I soon discovered that darts would stick into the soft acoustical ceiling tiles very easily. I had a dart board of course, but that was pretty boring. I would often lie on the playroom floor, my sword and shield and spear within easy reach, munching on my Viking Campfire Toast, staring up at the tiles, planning my next raid on an unsuspecting coastal village. Then one day, just for fun, I tossed a dart up into one of the tiles to see what would happen. It stuck for about five seconds and then detached itself and fell back towards the floor. But as it fell, I saw the the weighted pointy end turn downward, and watched, fascinated, as it it stuck straight up into the Indoor-Outdoor carpeting on the playroom floor. I was amazed and delighted. From there it was a natural progression, a boyish no-brainer equation. Darts, plus soft ceiling tiles, plus unsupervised free time, equals boyishly witless experimentation with potentially hazardous results. Which, actually, is a pretty good description of my entire childhood.

Thus, I invented The Dart Game. It seemed perfectly harmless at the time. I figured no one would notice a few more tiny holes in the classic 1960's style acoustical ceiling tiles since there were already thousands of them. So I would toss a dart up into the acoustical ceiling tiles and then see how long it took for it to fall back to the floor. The carpet showed no marks whatsoever so I was in good shape in terms of accountability. It was a simple variation of The Arrow Game. The dart goes up, sticks in the soft acoustical tiles for a few moments and then falls back down. It was Simple-Minded, and Classic, and I didn't even need a Football helmet to play it. I used some of my model tanks and plastic army guys as targets for the darts to land on. It was just about as much fun as I had ever had, and it didn't involve flames, or matches, or loud explosions either.

We had a solid heavy wooden ping pong table that was always set up in the middle of the playroom. One version of The Dart Game involved the ping pong table. My goal was to get the dart stuck in the acoustical tiles for a few moments as usual, and then watch it stick into the ping pong table as it fell from the ceiling. If the dart got stuck up in the ceiling tiles, I used my hockey stick to dislodge it. I had never played ice hockey, therefore, why I owned a hockey stick is still a mystery to me, but it sure came in handy. It had also served as a nice musket when I'd gone through a fairly intense Daniel Boone phase earlier in my childhood. And yes, I had a Coonskin Cap.

On the fateful day that will forever go down as one of the true low points of my entire life, the dart just wouldn't come free from the ceiling. It was stuck over the very center of the ping pong table, and I couldn't quite reach it with the hockey stick. So I climbed up onto the ping pong table and got right under the dart. I got *directly* under the dart. Just as I was reaching up with the hockey stick to dislodge the dart, it detached from the ceiling all by itself, and fell straight down, just like it always did.

I vividly remember every detail of that moment. I was standing *directly* under the dart looking up at it, still reaching up with my hockey stick to dislodge it. The whole sequence seemed to be happening in slow motion. First, the feathers were falling towards me, but while I stared upward in frozen fascination, the dart's weighted pointy end turned downwards very quickly, just like it always did. My brilliant reaction was to hunch my shoulders, scrunch my eyes closed, and make an expectant, unhappy facial expression. The dart hit me right in the middle of the top of my head. It made a fairly loud "*thwocking*" sound when it struck my skull. Like the sound that you make when you hit a piece of wood with your knuckles. "*Thwock!!*" But more importantly, it *really* hurt.

I dropped the hockey stick, grabbed at the dart and began kind of jumping around on the ping pong table. The hockey stick got tangled up in my legs, and in an effort to avoid it, I jumped sideways and landed on one corner of the ping pong table. The table leg under that corner gave way. That whole side of the table went down, and I went down with it. As I tumbled onto the carpeted floor the dart fell out of my head. As the ping pong table fell over, the corner of it smashed into the playroom wall and chopped a large triangular hole right through the sheetrock. A generalized crashing sound accompanied all of this. Apparently the acoustical tiles couldn't absorb something of this decibel magnitude, because my dad heard it up in the living room and came charging down the playroom stairs to see what had happened.

My Dad, Very Concerned,
"What happened!? Are you ok?!"

Me, Somewhat Dazed, But Still Alert,
"Yeah, Dad, I'm ok... ummm... I was trying to adjust the net on this side, and when I leaned on the table the leg just sort of collapsed... I guess."

This wasn't really very fair of me to be honest. My dad had built the ping pong table in his garage workshop as a Birthday present for me the year before. It was built like a battleship out of heavy plywood and 4x4 legs. No twelve year old on earth could have leaned on that thing and caused the legs to collapse. Well, maybe a twelve year old Apprentice Sumo Wrestler could have, maybe. Fortunately, the pointy end of the dart drew hardly any blood at all. I went upstairs to the bathroom and washed it out of my hair, and that was the only damage I sustained.

So my kindhearted and concerned dad spent the next day or two repairing the triangular shaped hole in the playroom wall and reinforcing the legs of the ping pong table. Of course this just made the ping pong table even sturdier which made that version of The Dart Game all that much safer to play. So I continued getting up early, going downstairs into the playroom to make my Viking Campfire Toast, and merrily tossing more darts up into the classic 1960's style acoustical ceiling tiles. No one ever noticed those few hundred more little holes, just like I figured.

Chapter 5

My Field Of Dreams: If You Burn It, They Will Come, Eventually

IN AUGUST, 1966, THE ENTIRE East Coast of The United States was in the middle of the worst drought in decades. I was in the middle of being thirteen, a dangerous age. Things were so dry by mid-summer that the long grass in the big hay field behind our house made crackling noises when I walked or ran through it. The big hay field was my main theater of outdoor operations during the warmer seasons. It was kind of a huge version of the playroom for me.

The big hay field was actually two fields separated by an old fashioned cattle lane that ran down the middle between them. About half of the right hand hay field was an old apple orchard. Our housing development was built on a former dairy farm, and about one hundred identical split level development houses stood on one hundred half acre plots where the dairy cows had once grazed. The two big hay fields were a buffer zone separating our recently built development houses from the big white colonial era house that stood across the way. It was a beautiful house with green doors and shutters, and the property had a tennis court, a pool, and a horse barn too. My back yard was aligned with the lane that ran between the fields so all I had to do was hop over the stone wall at the back of our yard, and I would immediately enter a wonderland of boyhood adventure. If only I had been normal.

Of course my friends and I made plenty of real campfires out in the big hay fields, and cooked hot dogs and hamburgers, while generally pretending that we were Backwoodsmen and Pioneers. It was the staging ground for some epic Viking Raids too. We also built some pretty serious log huts replete with sod roofs that were more like a little village actually. But I'm sorry to report that a friend and I also invented The Burning Grass Game. Like I said, if only I'd been normal.

I don't recommend The Burning Grass Game. It was what my parents would have called a Bad Idea if they had known about it. It was a very basic game that held endless fascination for us. Me and my best friend, Timmy, would wander around the field fluffing up little teepee shaped tufts of the bone-dry wispy grass, put a match under them and watch them flare up. Then we would stomp up and down on them so as to put the flames out right away and move on to our next grass teepee. We were always very careful about our stomping, but the truly low level of our intelligence is hard to believe looking back on it all.

On this particularly memorable day we were playing The Burning Grass Game about halfway across the hay field along the edge of a dry stream bed. This low lying area was about two hundred feet from the stone wall separating the hay fields from the white big Colonial era house with its tennis court and pool and horse barn. One of our friends, Olivia Johnson, lived in the big white Colonial era house. It was a bit like the Middle Ages or Pre-Revolutionary France. Olivia and her parents were like the landed aristocrats, and we were like the hard working peasants living in the little houses near the big chateau. Everyone seemed fine with this arrangement.

So in the middle of August, in the middle of my thirteenth year, in the middle of the worst drought in decades, there we were out in the middle of the big hay field happily fluffing up little grass teepees, lighting them with matches, and then stomping them out very contentedly that afternoon. We could hear the thwacking of tennis balls and could see a game of doubles under way at the Johnson's tennis court. A nice breeze had sprung up blowing towards the Johnson's side of the field. It felt refreshing in the oppressively dry summer heat. We finished stomping up and down on our most recent little flaming grass teepee and moved on to find another likely spot. It was a relaxing and lazy summer scene, but not for long.

The relaxation and laziness ended abruptly when we heard sharp crackling noises behind us. We turned around and saw that one of our little fluffed up grass teepees had re-ignited. We had stomped in vain. We reacted quickly to this alarming situation. We sprinted back to stomp it out again, but before we could do so, it came to life with the breeze fanning it. It took only a few seconds for it to become a low wall of hungry spreading flames. We grabbed some dead stalks of bracken lying nearby and tried to beat the flames out. We didn't see that with every backswing we were sending little bits and twigs of burning bracken off into the grass behind us. A host of little fires were springing up around us quicker than we could get to them. The little fires leapt to life all around us, and the small hungry wall of flame became a big hungry wall of flame moving at us from all sides. We were in danger of being totally surrounded and engulfed by the flames. Dropping our bundles of bracken we ran for our lives with the flames closing in. The roaring of the hungry flames rose behind us as we ran. This was serious.

Big clouds of smoke were now rolling across the field and wafting across the tennis court, pushed by the breeze blowing directly towards the Johnson's house. As we hurdled over the stone wall that separated the big hay field from the Johnson's back lawn, I could see the tennis players waving their hands in front of their faces to clear the smoke away as they bravely tried to play on. We fled for the house in total panic, and the tennis players began retreating off the court too. We pounded on the back door of the house. Mrs. Johnson eventually came to the door, and in an unhurried manner she asked us what all the commotion was about. We poured out our story, tripping over the words, pointing wildly back towards the encroaching flames. She calmly looked out past us and said,

"Oh my, yes... yes boys, it's certainly coming this way. My goodness."

We looked back and saw that the hungry flames were climbing over the stone wall, gaining new life from some big piles of dry leaves that were banked against it. This was now *seriously* serious. It looked like the fire was going to come right across the lawn and start on the barn, and the barn wasn't very far from the house. Mrs. Johnson calmly searched for the phone number of the Fire Department, dialed it, said a few words to whoever answered and included her address. Then she put down the receiver and spoke to us again,

"Don't worry boys, the Firemen are on their way. You two go out to the end of the driveway and wait for them. I'll get out the hose."

The *hose*? Yes, the hose. As Mrs. Johnson bravely prepared to face the oncoming inferno with her garden hose, we sprinted down to the end of the driveway to the main road to await the Fire Department. I felt like we were out in the Wild West awaiting the arrival of the Cavalry. I don't know how many minutes had passed, but the smoke was getting pretty thick up by the house, and we could see the tennis players fleeing towards their cars. I felt sick and scared. I never wanted to see another book of matches again as long as I lived. It felt like an eternity, but very soon, thankfully, we heard the Main Firehouse Siren start wailing out from afar, and I did my best not to cry from pure relief.

Our prayers were answered. Everything was going to be ok. The Johnson's barn and house were not going to burn to the ground because within like three minutes the First Responder Fireman Guy's car came speeding up the driveway. The car slid to a heroic stop in a proverbial cloud of dust with our Hero behind the wheel. And it was right around this point in time that my total faith in adults wafted away like the clouds of smoke from the burning hay field and never, *ever* returned.

Our heroic First Responder Fireman Guy had arrived on the scene in an un-heroic looking, dented up old Ford station wagon. It slid to a halt with a generalized clanking sound and some oily looking exhaust smoke trailing it up the driveway. We knew right away this wasn't going to be good. The inside of the car was a messy jumble of paint cans, tools, brushes, at least one step-ladder, and hopefully some First Responder Fireman Guy Gear. The First Responder Fireman Guy did not appear to be highly organized, or physically fit either. He slowly extracted himself from driver's side of the old Ford, fought his way into the back seat, and began slowly rummaging for his First Responder Fireman Guy Gear. And I repeat, *slowly*.

After a confused struggle during which he got one arm trapped in the rungs of the stepladder for a few desperate moments, he emerged with a short handled flimsy looking broom and a small tank of water that strapped on like a backpack. None of this happened quickly. His pants were falling below his ample waistline, but he was there, and he was a First Responder Fireman Guy after all. He began huffing and puffing up the driveway which had about a one degree incline, valiantly advancing towards the raging inferno with a ratty looking old broom and five gallons of water. We were dumbstruck by our ill-equipped savior. We still believed in the all powerful abilities of adults, and we certainly held Firemen in awe, but this was putting our faith to a severe test.

At the top end of the driveway the First Respond-er Fireman Guy met his first obstacle, Mrs. Johnson's climbing rose bushes. These were planted against three sections of white board fencing, three boards high, with posts about eight feet apart. The top edge of the top board was maybe three feet off the ground. The climbing rose bushes reached up gracefully out of a bed of neatly raked pine bark mulch. The deep red of the roses made a nice contrast against the white boards of the fence. If the First Responder Guy had walked 15 feet to either side, he could have simply gone around the fencing and continued on to the critical fire zone, but he *didn't* go around. He made straight for the climbing rose bushes and the white board fence, and we realized he was going to attempt to climb *over* the fence. I swear to you and hope to die, that this is really true. It was like the Desert Toll Booth scene in "Blazing Saddles".

Our plucky First Responder Fireman Guy trudged right across the neatly raked pine bark mulch, put one hand on the top board of the fence, and tried to swing his right leg over it. He gave a half hearted little hop which I guess was supposed to boost his leg up and over the top board, but he didn't make it. His large butt got stuck on the top board while his left foot scrambled in the loose mulch for some kind of boosting leverage. His foot slipped out from beneath him in the mulch, and his bulky weight came down heavily on the top board. It bowed downwards under him for a millisecond, and then gave way with a muffled, "Crack-*Snap*!". This was followed by two more, "Crack-*Snap*!, Crack-*Snap*!" sounds as he broke through the two lower boards in succession. They broke beneath him one after another, and he crashed onto the ground with a grunt among the climbing rose bushes and the neatly raked pine bark mulch. He came to rest there on the broken boards, legs splayed, stunned by his fall. The water tank was hanging off him, and his broom somewhere in the pile-up. We were more stunned than he was. Was this Our Town's Finest? Was this our savior, our heroic Real First Responder Fireman Guy, defeated by a three foot high board fence and some rose bushes? Yes, it was.

We really didn't know what to do. We took a few hesitant steps towards the downed First Responder Fireman Guy, but then we heard Fire Truck sirens out on the main road. Once again we felt an enormous wave of hope. The *Real* Fire Trucks were on their way with *Really Real* Firemen Guys. We abandoned the First Responder Fireman Guy to his fate among climbing roses and the mulch and sprinted down to the end of the driveway again.

And there they were. The *Real* Thing, the *Real* Fire Department, roaring down the main road straight towards us in three *Real* Fire Trucks and two Specially Equipped *Real* Fire Department Pickup Trucks. And there were lots of Real Fireman Guys hanging off of the trucks too. I think I started to cry a little bit again when we saw them. But then our faith in grownups took another severe blow. One after another, without any warning, the *Real* Fire Trucks hung a hairy left hand turn about three hundred yards up the road *before* the Johnson's driveway and disappeared into our development's main entrance. We realized in a flash that they were going the *wrong way* to gain access to the burning field. I think my brain stopped functioning for a few seconds, really. But Timmy's brain was still functioning, thank goodness. He jumped up in the air waving his arms and yelled,

"*Hey!!!... Over Here!!!!*"

Timmy yelled those words louder than any human being has ever yelled, before or since. And the very last Real Fireman Guy hanging off of the very last Real Fire Truck heard him, somehow. I started jumping up and down and shouting too. That very last truck stopped, backed up, and came roaring towards us again with the rest of the fleet backing and turning and following right after it. They came flying up the driveway and deployed for action just like they did in the movies. Meanwhile, our poor First Responder Fireman Guy was still down on the ground struggling manfully with his gear and the broken boards. He was still tangled up in those pesky climbing rose bushes, and they were getting the better of him.

So the cavalry actually arrived, better late than never, and put out the fire in about five minutes. The crisis was over, and all was well. The Johnson's house and barn were safe. Everything had happened so fast, and things were still moving quickly. The Real Fireman Guys were gathering up their gear and winding up the big hoses, getting ready to turn their trucks around to head back to the Firehouse. The main Fireman Guy was speaking with Mrs. Johnson by her back door. He was asking her if she knew how the fire had started. This wasn't good, but I knew that my moment had come. It was all my fault. I was ready to confess my crime and take my punishment. I walked over and tugged on his arm. He turned an expectant gaze my way. It was a pivotal, life altering conversation for me.

Main Fireman Guy, Condescendingly Friendly,

"Yes, son?"

Me, With New Found Totally Honest Boyish Conviction,

"Well, um, you see, Sir, we were playing in the field...."

Main Fireman Guy, With Sober Patronizing Approval,

"Yes, Mrs. Johnson told me all about it. You boys did the right thing. You two did a Good Deed. You probably saved the barn and the house too. Running up here and alerting Mrs. Johnson was very brave of you. That field was going up in flames fast! Good job. Good work. We need more responsible kids around here like you two. Well done!"

Me, Desperately Attempting To Confess,

"But sir... you see... we were playing in the field..."

Main Fireman Guy, Kindly Dismissing Me,

"You boys have had a tough afternoon, why don't you go on home now? Everything is all right now. Good job. Good work."

He wasn't going to let me tell the truth. He wasn't listening to a word I was saying. He patted me on the shoulders in a comforting manner and repeated,

"Good job, good job..."

And that was it. The conversation was over. My big moment to redeem myself had come and gone with less effect than the First Responder Fireman Guy's comical attempt to hurdle the white fence. The Main Fireman Guy climbed into the front seat of one of the pick up trucks, gave us a cheerful wave, and drove off down the driveway. We stood there staring as the trucks disappeared one by one. I don't know what Timmy was thinking, but I was seeing grown-ups in a brand new light like when I found out Santa Claus wasn't real. We said goodbye to Mrs. Johnson and headed back across the semi-destroyed hay field towards our homes. We made a wide circle around the burned area. It looked like an entire quarter of the field had been torched. When we got to my back yard, my dad was there staring across the field towards the burnt section over by the Johnson's house.

My Dad, Concerned,

"Boy, that was some fire out there, huh? You boys know how that fire got started? Are you both ok?"

Me, Surrendering To The Inevitable,

"Yeah Dad, we're ok. We were playing out in the field and saw the flames start up and so we ran to the house to tell Mrs. Johnson..."

My Dad, With Approval,

"You did the right thing. That was a good deed. You probably saved the barn and the house and who knows what else. That was very responsible and grown up of you."

Me, Resigned To My Fate,

"Thanks Dad, the Fireman said the same thing to us. We're just glad everything turned out ok, *right* Timmy?"

Timmy gave me a knowing look and trudged off towards his house. The truth about that fire would remain our shared secret, but this was the turning point for me. I swore off my pyrotechnic ways, cold turkey, right then and there. The cruel irony was how my attempt at a heartfelt confession had fallen on deaf ears. I would happily go back to stabbing couch cushions, shooting arrows into the sky, and sticking darts in my head. I might even crash my bike into a parked car for old time's sake, but I was totally and finally done with the whole fire thing.

Chapter 6

The Girl In The Pool

THAT FATEFUL SUMMER ROLLED RELENTLESS-
LY forward, and the upcoming school year
began to make its presence felt. I continued
to pursue my Viking Raids and play with my friends,
but it just wasn't the same anymore. Viking Toast
was off limits to me now. I cringed when I saw my
dad's gasoline can in the garage, and I stayed as far
away from our outdoor charcoal grill as possible. I
only used Elmer's Glue for any projects, because the
sight and smell of rubber cement scared me. I still
acted out various imaginary Pioneer and Back-
woodsman scenes in the big hay field, but I stayed
away from the area where the fire had happened. It
seemed like I had actually learned from my mistakes.

About two weeks after the incident in the hay
field my mom invited several of her friends over to
our house for an afternoon of gossip and swimming
in our back yard pool. September was only a couple

of weeks away, and summer was quickly coming to a close. I was wise enough to steer clear of my mom and her women friends by staying in the house, but it was another hot summer day, and we didn't have air conditioning in those days. From my bedroom window I could look out on the back yard and the pool area which was enclosed by a 5 ft high chain link fence. All swimming pools had to have a fence around them to keep pets and kids and wildlife from falling into them. I contemplated going into the pool for a nice cool swim in spite of the Gossip Circle out there, but I wasn't sure if it was worth it.

I was getting really bored being cooped up in the house. My room had no cross ventilation, and the disturbing odor of decayed rabbit was painfully evident on days like this. I stared blankly down at the scene by the pool. The ladies were all talking together with their lounge chairs pulled up in a tight circle just outside of the pool fence. One of them had brought her eighteen month old daughter with her, but there were no other kids on hand. I casually observed that the gate to the pool was open, and then I noticed that the little girl was walking towards the open gate. She was carrying a doll under her arm, and no one was paying any attention to her. In a flash of unusually heightened awareness I saw exactly what was going to happen. My mom and the other women were absorbed in their chatty conversation. They didn't notice the girl heading towards the edge of the pool.

Somehow, and I don't really know how or why, I knew with total certainty that she was going to walk right off the edge of the pool and fall into the water. I just knew it. I didn't hesitate, or wait around up in my room to see if it would come true, I turned away from the window and started running.

I ran out of my room, down the stairs into the living room, down the stairs into the playroom, and kept running straight out the playroom door. As I burst out onto the back lawn I saw the little girl step right off the edge of the pool and drop straight down into the water without uttering a sound or making much of a splash either. It happened exactly as I had thought. None of the ladies were aware that the girl had fallen into the pool. I kept running right past their circle of lawn chairs and through the gate of the pool fence. They were all still busily chatting and didn't even notice me. I stopped at the edge of the pool and looked down. I will never, *ever,* forget what I saw.

The little girl was lying face up on the bottom of the shallow end of the pool in about three feet of water. She was lying perfectly still, except her blond hair was moving with the current of water coming from the filter vent. Her blue eyes were open, staring up at me through the crystal clear water, and bubbles were coming out of her mouth. She wasn't even struggling. I jumped into the water, gathered her up in my arms and came surging up out of the water again, all in about two seconds. I climbed out of the pool with her in my arms. Water was streaming off of us and splashing all around. The girl was still clutching her doll tightly in her arms. She spit out some water and started crying, more of a wailing sound than a crying sound, and that was the first moment that any of those ladies knew that anything out of the ordinary had happened. Everything became total pandemonium for a few minutes with me and the girl dripping water, the girl wailing like crazy, and the girl's mom freaking out.

The ladies all gathered around making a huge amount of noise. The girl's mom grabbed her from me, and then they all gathered around her leaving me standing there alone, dripping, and soaked. I had saved her life, and the whole thing had happened in less than a minute from the time I had first spotted her walking towards the edge of the pool and the moment when the moms all realized what had happened. I was a total Hero all the way. I had finally, really, actually, done a Good Deed.

From that point on, as far as my parents were concerned, I could do no wrong. I had completely confirmed their erroneous opinion of me. I had bumbled my way into fulfilling their beliefs. I had confirmed beyond a shadow of a doubt that I was Amazing. I was Hugely Mature. I was Wise Beyond My Years. I could spot Trouble from a distance and literally leap to the Rescue. They thought I could Do

No Wrong, when in fact I could Do No Right for as long as I could remember.

In terms of my new found status, I was the only one who knew none of it was true, but just like the Main Fireman Guy, no one wanted to listen. Although, to be honest, I didn't really try to change the positive view of me that everyone now had. I was enjoying being looked upon as a responsible and sensible young man. Then about a week later my mom asked me a fateful question. It seemed non-prophetic and innocent at the time. My answer turned out to be the single most important answer to any question that anyone has ever asked me in my entire life. That answer became the Guiding Star of the whole rest of my life even though I didn't know it at the time. As usual, I had virtually no idea what I was getting myself into.

My Mom, Patronizingly Respectful,

"We want to send you to Sleep Away Camp next July. You deserve it after the great things you did this summer helping with the fire at Johnson's and saving the little girl in the pool. Would you like to go to Canoeing Camp or Riding Camp? It's your decision, you're old enough to know what's best for you now."

Me, Bewildered, As Usual,

"Well... ummm... I guess I'd like to learn about horses and riding and stuff, you know... I mean... so... Riding Camp, please."

And that one answer to that one question changed everything for me and influenced the entire course of the rest of my life. At the time I had no idea that the following summer I would meet incredible new friends and have new experiences that would make my early years seem tame by comparison. In my mind summer camp was going to be a carefully controlled environment supervised by fully fledged, responsible and reasonable grown-ups. It had a restful appeal to me after the close calls with disaster that I had somehow survived. I was really looking forward to it and began to learn about horses and riding gear and all the stuff that went with it.

All I had to do was get myself safely through the next ten months. With school starting up again I would have less time to get into dangerous situations on my own at home. Things looked good. But this was also the year I would enter 8th Grade which meant I would attend our town's Junior High School and meet kids from other Middle Schools. I was looking forward to making new friends. What I didn't know was that this was going to be the year I would become best friends with one of the most unusual and fascinating people I would ever meet. I was about to become a willing disciple of the all time Jedi Master of Classroom Mayhem, the Crown Prince of Academic Disruption, the one and only Jack McCormack. I didn't know that it was going to be a very, very *educational* year in more ways than I could ever imagine.

Chapter 7

Cry Havoc! And Let Loose The Dogs of 8th Grade

I N SPITE OF ALL MY lame-brained misadventures and total lack of practical common sense, I was still what you would call a Good Boy. I unwittingly stuck the dart in my *own* head as you will recall, I didn't try to hurt anyone else with it. My other escapades were similar in that there was never any direct intention on my part to set fire to things or destroy anyone's property. All that stuff happened by accident. I was just a clueless kid stumbling through my pre-adolescence, and it's a miracle I got through it in one piece.

Jack McCormack, my new best friend in Junior High School, wasn't really a Bad Boy, but he wasn't completely a Good Boy either. He approached school in a way that was utterly new to me. He had a different view of what school had to offer. He wasn't what adults back then would call a Juvenile Delinquent, but he more or less made a career out of relentlessly testing the patience and fortitude of our teachers. He was full of ideas and energy, and his intentions were to disrupt, distract, unhinge, frustrate, and otherwise get under the skin of our Junior High School teachers every chance he got. He had a knack for seeing those opportunities everywhere, everyday, all day. And to top it all off, he was really funny, I mean *hysterically* funny through all of it.

On the first day of 8th Grade we arrived at our town's Junior High School by bus and were all sent directly into the gym to be given our Homeroom assignments. The teachers were sitting behind long tables busily giving out our Homeroom Classroom numbers and issuing us name tags. I didn't quite understand what all the commotion was about and found myself shuffling along in line right behind a big strapping boy wearing an army jacket, blue jeans, and work boots. I was wearing nice pants and a buttoned down collared shirt. I also wore thick glasses, had a roundish face, and blond hair that was almost white from the summer's sun. The big boy in front of me was at least a head taller than I was and taller than most everyone else too. He turned towards me, looked down at my name tag, and remarked,

"So, *Mr. Eric Hill*, you look like something from a Norman Rockwell painting, did your Mom dress you this morning?"

I really didn't know what to say. I couldn't tell if he was kidding me in a friendly way or making fun of me for real, and he was kind of big and kind of rough looking. I stared at him blankly for a moment, blinking like an owl behind my thick glasses, and words just wouldn't come to me. I probably looked scared, and I had no idea how to respond. Suddenly, he let out a big laugh, slapped me on the back, and said,

"*Oh Man*! You're going to need a body guard in this place if you go around looking like that! I will take it upon myself to protect you from the dangers of this dreaded old Junior High School. Who's Home-room are you in?"

I stammered out, "Mrs. Tr... Tr... Tromler's..."

He whomped me on the back again, gave a big horsey laugh, and said in a loud and amused voice,

"Me too! I hear she's a tough one! We'll have to see what kind of stuff she's made of. So, its Eric right? Like, Eric The Red? Are you some kind of Viking?"

This hit a bit too close to home for me, and for some reason I responded by imitating his casual boisterous attitude. In a sarcastic tone I replied,

"Yeah, that's right, I'm Eric The Red. I just got back from discovering Greenland and boy are my arms killing me from all that rowing..."

Jack let out another huge horsey laugh, slapped me again on the back, and declared,

"I like you, Eric The Red. I am dubbing us Best Friends from now on, and we're in the same Homeroom! Let's go have some fun with mean old Mrs. Tr... Tr... Tromler!"

I soon found out that Jack saw each school day as an endless series of amusing opportunities to have fun at the expense of our teachers. He also had a knack for getting other kids to join in on his schemes and shenanigans. His energy and enthusiasm were hard to resist. He was honorable and loyal, and when confronted with his transgressions, which was fairly often, he did not shift the blame to anyone else. He accepted his punishment, yet he would almost always turn the punishment into another opportunity to create more chaos. He believed that no punishment should go unpunished. He was smart, tall, strong, athletic, good looking, and fully committed to being the biggest thorn in the side of any teacher he found to be unworthy of educating us. For our 8th grade year his disapproval fell partially on our Homeroom and Social Studies teacher, Mrs. Tromler, but his all time Nemesis became our rookie Shop Teacher, Mr. Prine. For Jack and Mr. Prine it was war at first sight.

Jack had determination and perseverance. He never gave up on a project or idea once he made up his mind to move forward with it. Take, for example, his four month long crusade to puncture a hole in the top of every mountain on earth. We had a plastic relief map of the world that took up one wall of our

Homeroom, and it was the pride and joy of Mrs. Tromler. She loved to stand next to it and point out various geographic locations in various parts of the world with her wooden chalk holder-pointer thing. She had to use the pointer thing because, unfortunately, Mrs. Tromler was a tad under five feet tall even in her stubby dark brown teacher shoes with the one inch heels. Jack was about 5'10" at age fourteen, and I think he was already shaving too. Jack had long arms that enabled him to reach out and create trouble a seat or two away from him, and he was nimble on his feet.

In Math we were doing basic Geometry for which we all had a Protractor and a Compass. Our Compasses were the old fashioned metal kind, and they had an incredibly dangerous needle-sharp pointy end. Those compasses just begged to be stuck into things. We did plenty of tattooing of various wooden surfaces throughout the school. We also routinely punctured our hardcover books with them. Who wouldn't? Jack spotted the plastic relief map of the world on the first day of our Homeroom and Social Studies classes. He claimed a seat at the back of the row that ran along the side of the classroom next to the map. I sat with him because he was fun to be around and always up to something. He leaned towards me, and in a hushed tone he vowed to poke a hole in the top of *every mountain on earth,* and I just knew he meant it.

His seat location also positioned him right by Mrs. Tromler's big closet at the back of the classroom where she stored her supplies and kept the Holy Grail of our Social Studies class, The New York Times. The Times was a huge deal for Mrs. Tromler. Each morning when Homeroom ended she would proceed to the back of the closet and ceremonially emerge burdened with an armful of the Times. She would then select one of us to help her hand them out for the first part of Social Studies class.

She should have enlisted Jack's help rather than leave him unsupervised while she was preoccupied in the closet. On about our third day of class Mrs. Tromler went into the closet to get the Times. The Supply Closet was maybe eight feet deep and about six feet wide. It had double doors that opened outward and locked from the outside. When the doors were open, one side was within reach of Jack's very long arms. So when Mrs. Tromler walked in towards the back of the closet, Jack got a conspiratorial look on his face and went into a big theatrical yawn. He stretched his arms out wide and flicked the open door lightly with his fingers. The door swung shut slowly, gently, and silently. It closed with a slight "*snick*" which meant it was firmly locked. Mrs. Tromler was locked in her own classroom's Supply Closet, and Jack hadn't even gotten out of his seat.

The whole class stared at the closed and locked Supply Closet door. Jack put his fingers to his lips to signal us all to be quiet. The silence was immediately shattered when Mrs. Tromler began pounding on the inside of the door, screeching to be let out.

Thud!, Bam!!, Thud!!! "Let me out!!!"

The toes of her chunky dark brown teacher shoes were protruding from under the edge of the door kind of like how the Wicked Witch's shoes stuck out from beneath Dorothy's house after she crash landed in Oz. Mrs. Tromler had a very high pitched voice when she was mad or frustrated. In this case she was mad *and* frustrated so she was screeching like crazy,

"*Let me out*! *Somebody open this door right now*! *Let me out*!"

And of course it was Jack who jumped up, opened the door, switched on the light, and rescued Mrs. Tromler. Then he assisted her with the Times, gently guiding her to her desk and making lots of sympathetic noises, fussing like a mother hen. Poor Mrs. Tromler didn't know that Jack was going to have enormous amounts of fun with the Supply Closet and the Times all year long. He had been merely testing the waters to see what was possible for the future, and the future looked bright.

Jack's plan for the big plastic relief map was ambitious and inspiring. Each morning during our Homeroom period he would sit impassively at his desk, seeming to be the perfect student. But every time Mrs. Tromler would turn her back to us in order to write something on the black board, or whenever she would look down at the papers on her desk, Jack would go to work on that map. He would intently puncture as many mountaintops as he could in the brief time he had, using the needle sharp pointy end of his compass. He would continue this diligent work all during Social Studies too. It was awe inspiring to see him working at it, but after the first week he ran out of mountaintops that were within his reach.

Mrs. Tromler seated her students in a ranked order of attentiveness, enthusiasm, participation in class discussion, and grades. The better students sat up front. Jack started at the back of the room because in 7th Grade he'd had a reputation for non-participation, lack of interest, and mediocre grades. He could only achieve his dream of puncturing a hole in top of every mountain on earth if he could gain access to the rest of the map. And he could only gain access to the rest of the map if he could shift his seat towards the front row by improving his class ranking. He could only improve his ranking by getting better grades, participating effectively in class discussions, and generally upgrading his academic image, and that was exactly what he did.

Jack's gradual transformation into the, "Boy Scout, Goody Two Shoes Social Studies Student", was a work of art by a true master. He was a goal oriented kid, and he made a genuine effort to do well in the class so that he could move gradually up towards the front of his row. These gradual promotions gave him access to more of the map, and more of the mountain tops. He punctured tiny holes in all those peaks over the course of four months and got a B+ in the class for the first semester too. Projects like puncturing every mountaintop on Earth were fun for Jack, a form of amusement and play, but his out and out war with our first year Shop Teacher, Mr. Prine, was all business.

Chapter 8

Yellow Wood Glue And The Paddle

M R. PRINE AND JACK TOOK one look at each other at the beginning of our first term of 8th Grade Shop class, and I knew it was going to be a very long year for Mr. Prine, assuming he lasted that long. Mr. Prine wore bow ties, a sure sign of eccentricity, and he was one of those teachers who loved to exercise authority merely to prove he could. He was skinny and wore bookish looking black rimmed glasses and had one of those long necks with an Adam's Apple that bobbed up and down when he spoke. To make matters worse he had a manner of speech that really irritated us, and Jack became adept at imitating it right away.

Mr. Prine addressed us as if we knew absolutely nothing, and he knew absolutely everything. He used phrases that were intended to make him seem witty and clever, but he had a terrible sense of timing. He thought he needed to establish his authority right away, and this was the kind of challenge that Jack never backed down from, *ever*. Our other Shop teacher, Mr. Chandler, was a seasoned veteran who knew how to avoid useless interpersonal challenges of this nature. Jack sensed the difference and immediately approved of Mr. Chandler which made his immediate *disapproval* of Mr. Prine more acute.

One day during our second week of 8th Grade Shop class Mr. Prine directed us to take our places at our pre-assigned seats set around six heavy wooden Shop Tables. Tall wooden shop stools were set around each table. Each shop table had a big vise at each corner and a recessed center section that held pencils, tape measures, T-squares, and quart-size soft plastic bottles of Yellow Wood Glue. These bottles had wide mouths with screw-on caps and tapered application cones similar to the Ketchup and Mustard bottles in the cafeteria, only much larger. Of course Mr. Prine cautioned us about the Yellow Wood Glue bottles in his irritatingly patronizing manner,

"You must all be very, *very careful* when you are pouring out the glue, because it comes out very, *very fast*."

I saw Jack eyeing the Yellow Wood Glue bottles with that crafty look of his, and I knew he was cooking up something disruptive that involved them. We took our seats as directed. Mr. Prine handed out workbooks called Units to each of us. Each Shop period started with the class reading a Unit which was a one page lesson in Wood Shop basics. Then we had to answer multiple-choice questions based upon the reading. As everyone bent down to read their Units, I saw one of Jack's long arms snake out and snatch a bottle of the Yellow Wood glue back into his lap. He never raised his head. We were all reading under Mr. Prine's watchful eye, but I could see that Jack was unscrewing the cap of the bottle with his free hand. Mr. Prine turned his attention elsewhere for a moment. Still without raising his head, Jack lobbed the bottle of Yellow Wood Glue onto another table about ten feet away.

The soft plastic bottle of Yellow Wood Glue landed with a loud "*thwump!!*" followed by a gurgley, sloppy "*blurp*!!" sound. Everyone jumped in surprise. Yellow Wood Glue had splurped out of the bottle where it had landed on the table and was making a slowly widening gooey puddle that engulfed one of the Unit books and some pencils. Mr. Prine pounced on the boys at the table. He raised his voice sharply,

"I told you to be *careful*! Who did this?! Why did anyone *touch* the glue? We're doing *Units*! This *whole* table has to stay behind and *clean* this up!"

Jack stared at Mr. Prine impassively. One of his greatest skills was to appear completely expressionless when teachers began to freak out. He shook his head in mock disapproval. He pointed an accusing finger at our friends at the other table and scolded them in an exact imitation of Mr. Prine's speech pattern,

"You disobedient little *fellows*, look at the monumental *mess* you have made! For *shame*!"

This obvious personal mockery brought a look of determined outrage to Mr. Prine's pinched face, exactly as Jack had intended. Mr. Prine pointed his own long bony finger at Jack and delivered a warning,

"McCormack, don't become friends with *The Paddle* during your second week of Shop Class."

We all knew this was a serious threat. On the wall of the Shop was The Paddle. We had heard about The Paddle from other kids who had been to Shop class in previous years. It hung on the wall facing the entrance door to the Shop and looked like an oversized wooden Ping Pong paddle with sets of initials carved into the surface of it. These were the initials of the boys who had met the business end of The Paddle at the hands of Mr. Chandler or Prine's predecessor, Mr. Bergman.

Back then the Shop teachers were allowed to hit recalcitrant boys on the butt with The Paddle kind of like how they used to flog sailors in the British Navy. The teachers would hand down the sentence with a solemn foreboding look. Then the culprit would stand facing one of the shop tables with his hands on the table, and Mr. Chandler or Mr. Bergman would give him a pretty good whack or two with The Paddle. According to recipients of this old fashioned form of punishment, it could be fairly painful and the public nature of the punishment was embarrassing. But Jack saw it as just another opportunity to have some fun and to turn things around on Mr. Prine. We figured Mr. Prine was at the front end of another one of Jack's funny dramatic scenes that could only end in a bad way for the teacher. We shook our heads as we watched Mr. Prine fall right into the trap without even putting up a fight. It was a little sad to watch it unfold even though it was really, really funny. But first, some background history is in order.

One of Jack's really funny fail-proof set pieces of Disruptive Classroom Comedy involved what were called Pink Slips. Teachers handed you a Pink Slip when you were ejected from class, and then they sent you down to the Principal's office with it. I had never gotten one. Jack got a Pink Slip early in the year from most of his teachers, but they abandoned that tactic pretty quickly due to his creative theatrical urges. Our Principal was Mr. Fascinelli, a decent man who understood kids like Jack, but he was a no-nonsense administrator and was not reluctant to Suspend students or give out stiff Detentions. But as usual for Jack, a Pink Slip was just the kind of game he loved to play. We saw him perform his Pink Slip act enough times to learn the routine, and it never failed to create a comedic uproar. In the end, his teachers would realize that it was less disruptive to keep Jack in the classroom then to throw him out of it with a Pink Slip.

The Pink Slip routine had a predictable sequence. First, Jack would provoke the teacher into sending him to Mr. Fascinelli's office, usually by purposefully giving silly or inverted answers to the teacher's questions. For example, the teacher might ask,

"What position does Nikita Kruschev currently hold in the government of the Soviet Union?"

Jack would eagerly wave his hand around and make *"call on me!"* noises until he got called upon. That is to say, he would get called upon for the first two or three classes, but after that the teacher knew not to provide him with center stage. Once called upon, Jack would answer with a straight face and affected sincerity, something like,

"Nikita Kruschev currently holds the position of 'Outside Linebacker' in the Soviet Government, having recently been moved from his usual position of 'Nose Tackle'."

Or he might say,

"Nikita Kruschev currently holds the position of 'Head of Choreography', or, 'Director of Veterinary Research', or, 'Keeper of The Sacred Flame'."

The possibilities were endless, and we loved every minute of it. When he really got on a roll, Jack would add the word "toilet" to his answers. "Toilet", was the

Atomic Bomb of 8th Grade humor as far as we were concerned. It never failed to just kill us. So Jack would say,

"Nikita Krushchev currently holds the position of 'Head of *Toilet* Choreography', or 'Head Of Veterinary *Toilet* Research', or 'Keeper Of The Sacred *Toilet*'."

The teachers just hated it. Inevitably Jack would get called up to the teacher's desk, handed a Pink Slip, and be told sternly something along the lines of,

"Get out! Go to Mr. Fascinelli's office right now! Leave my classroom!"

Depending on Jack's mood this would go in one of several well rehearsed directions. Sometimes, he would fall down on his knees and beg abjectly for the teacher to reconsider. This begging usually included invoking his mother and father, his aunts and uncles, and his inevitable reference to,

"My sainted Irish Grandmother... may she rest in peace."

He would always say that, and then he would cross himself while piously gazing upward. We all knew Jack's grandmother was very much alive, and we also knew she was very much Italian too, so this was always entertaining. If begging didn't reverse his ejection, he would adopt a crushed and forlorn expression and then walk on his knees all the way out the classroom door. He would continue walking on his knees down the hall, leaving us in tears and the classroom in a shambles.

But my favorite ejection scenario was what we called "The Foot In The Wastebasket" routine. This was classically simple physical comedy. Jack would accept his ejection with seeming meekness and turn dejectedly to walk out the door. On his first step towards the door he would purposefully put his foot into the round metal wastebasket that was always positioned next to the teacher's desk. Jack's feet were about a size 10, and he always wore work boots not sneakers. So he would step down into the wastebasket, get it stuck on his boot, and then go clanking across the room as if it wasn't stuck to his foot at all. Of course the teacher would start to freak out and yell at him, and then he would get all panicky trying to shake the wastebasket off of his foot. This led to him falling down on his back while desperately trying to kick the wastebasket off, papers flying, arms flailing about, and generally appearing to be helplessly snared by the wastebasket. He was only just warming up.

Eventually, with a lot of bowing and scraping and many heartfelt apologies to the teacher, he would extract his foot, pick up the scattered papers, put the waste basket back in place, and resume his dejected march towards the door. But when he got to the door he would do "The Door In The Face" trick. This was yet another well rehearsed scenario that would always bring down the house, and Jack too. The trick was performed by putting the toe of his big work boot just ahead of the vertical plane of his nose, and then yanking the door open really hard. All the classroom doors opened inward. The door would hit the toe of his boot with a loud "Bang!". Upon impact Jack would grab his face with both hands, crying out in mock pain, and fall backwards onto the floor writhing around like crazy, crying out,

"Oh! Oh! My *nose*! My *nose*!"

It was very realistic looking. It required precision and timing which Jack always had in ample supply. Eventually, he would drag himself slowly out of the classroom, nursing his supposedly injured nose, and head down the hall to Mr. Fascinelli's office. The entire performance would leave the teacher steaming mad and us in total hysterics. We loved it. The teachers *really* hated it.

Therefore, on that fateful day in Shop class when Mr. Prine threatened him with the The Paddle, it offered Jack a similar opportunity to escalate things in his own comedic style. Much to Mr. Prine's surprise Jack hopped off of his shop stool and stood up to Mr. Prine, looking down at him with a defiant leer. Being a tall and fairly well built kid, most teachers found him a bit intimidating, but not Mr. Prine. Using Mr. Prine's exact cadence and voice inflection, Jack spoke out heatedly,

"What? My *good man*, are you threatening me with The Paddle? Do your *worst*, Mr. Prine! I *fear* you not! I *defy* you!"

We were shocked by this confrontation. I remember thinking that he had taken this too far, too fast, and that it did not look good for Jack. Mr. Prine took the bait and said,

"You *asked* for it McCormack, *assume* the position!"

Jack appeared to be cowed by Mr. Prine's superior tone. His defiant demeanor disappeared, his shoulders sagged, and the fight seemed to go out of him. He stood obediently with his back to Mr. Prine, facing our shop table, his hands gripping the table's edge. Mr. Prine took the paddle down and called to Mr. Chandler,

"Mr. Chandler, we have our *first* Paddle Friend!"

Mr. Chandler walked over and said soothingly,

"Now, now,... let's not be hasty Mr. Prine, it's so early in the year."

But Mr. Prine had drawn the proverbial line in the sand, and he was determined to establish his mastery over Jack. We couldn't believe that Mr. Prine didn't see the direction this was heading in. We knew that Jack never allowed a punishment to go unpunished, and we also knew that Mr. Prine didn't know this. Mr. Prine may have sensed that somehow he was making a mistake, but he couldn't back down now. He stepped up, and pulled back the paddle like Babe

Ruth stepping up to bat at home plate. He gave Jack only a half-hearted whack on the butt, more or less going through the motions without really trying to make it hurt. He might as well have swung as hard as he could, because the results were the same.

The moment the paddle touched the back pockets of his jeans, Jack let out a blood curdling bellow of mock pain and threw himself up and onto the table as if the force of the blow had sent him there. He kept his momentum going and rolled across the top of the table crashing to the floor on the other side. On his way across the top of the table his long arms swept everything off of it. Pencils, Unit books, Yellow Wood Glue bottles, rulers, a T-square or two, and a couple of tape measures all went flying. Then he rolled off the table, crashed onto the floor, and proceeded to writhe around in the sawdust grasping his butt and moaning in fake agony. This just killed us, and we all went nuts laughing our heads off. Mr. Prine stood there frozen in place with The Paddle still in his hands, but Jack wasn't finished. He crawled back around the table on his hands and knees to where Mr. Prine was still standing. Weeping and crying, he grabbed at the bottom edge of Mr. Prine's shop coat in supplication. He clutched the fabric in his hands and kissed the hem of the shop coat like Mr. Prine was the Pope or something. In his best broken voice he begged him to be merciful,

"Oh, dear Lord in Heaven, please, *please* Mr. Prine! I'll be a good boy from now on! I swear on the grave of my sainted Irish Grandmother... may she rest in peace..."

Of course with those words he paused, looked upwards, and crossed himself with a pious expression, then went back to the pleading and hysterics.

"Oh! Oh! The *pain*! The *pain*! Dear Lord, *please* don't hit me with *The Paddle* again!"

Mr. Chandler looked on with a resigned and knowing expression. I wondered if he almost sided with Jack on this one. Mr. Prine opened his mouth to speak, but then he placed the Paddle on top of the newly clean swept table and stalked out of the Shop in stony silence. In the awkward hush that followed Mr. Prine's dramatic exit, Mr. Chandler said sternly,

"Alright, McCormack, give it a rest. I think we've seen enough of your antics for one day. Clean up this mess, carve your initials into the Paddle, and go to your next class. Although, in my opinion, a love tap like that doesn't really qualify for the initials. Wait for the next time when you really get whacked. It shouldn't be very long from now I would guess. Just go to your next class, please."

I thought for a second or two that it looked like Mr. Chandler had to fight back a smile when he said this. We all knew Jack had won Round One, and we also knew that Mr. Prine could not be saved by the bell in this epic battle for supremacy. The only person who didn't know this was Mr. Prine himself, at least not just yet.

Chapter 9

The World's Smallest Tidal Wave, The Horn Of Plenty, and The Mountain Of Snow

JACK'S FEUD WITH MR. PRINE developed into a never ending war of the wills which always ended badly for Mr. Prine. Every other week or so Jack would pull some stunt or practical joke and get Paddled for it, but he clearly felt it was all worth it. Mr. Prine was a tough nut to crack as it turned out. He was made of sterner stuff than it seemed from just looking at him. I have been leery of teachers wearing bow ties ever since. You can't depend upon them to behave like normal teachers in certain situations. We all figured it was only a matter of time before Jack achieved total victory, but it was taking longer than we had expected.

I recall vividly the day in mid-winter when Jack snuck into the Shop a few minutes before class in order to create what he called "The World's Smallest

Tidal Wave". There was a small bathroom in the Shop. Jack went into it before the start of our class and wadded-up several paper towels that he used to plug up the sink in the bathroom. He turned on one of the faucets a little bit and left it running, of course, so the sink would eventually overflow. But he had also stuffed more wet paper towels under the bottom edge of the bathroom door where it met the floor. He had worked this out very carefully. This tactic gradually created a mini-lake on the bathroom floor once the sink overflowed. The mini-lake was just waiting to be set free by the first person who pulled open the bathroom door. When Mr. Prine arrived, the first thing he noticed was the sound of the faucet running in the bathroom, and naturally he yanked open the door to see what was going on inside. Immediately, a mini-tidal wave about an inch high came sweeping across the floor, right over his shoes, and out onto the Shop floor.

Mr. Prine couldn't prove that the mini-tidal wave was Jack's work, but his suspicions were pretty clear. He knew that we all knew who had done it. Without any explanation or attempt to find the culprit, Jack and I were chosen out of hand to mop up the floor under Mr. Prine's stern glance. The fact that Mr. Prine included me did not sit well with Jack, but he didn't argue or become theatrical. Instead he became very quiet and seemed absorbed in his thoughts. We mopped up the water and while we were putting the mops and buckets away, Jack said to me, in a low voice devoid of emotion,

"I'm tired of this guy, he's no fun anymore."

I knew this was not good. When a teacher "stopped being fun", Jack could get really difficult. On this particular day we had a session of Automotive Shop which was normally Jack's favorite area of interest. During our Auto Shop sessions he was always a model student. He loved cars and engines, and Mr. Prine actually knew a lot about them too. Mr. Prine regularly participated in weekend Road Rallies piloting his pride and joy, a 1963 MGB convertible that was in the traditional Hunter Green color. This was a two seater sports car that even had the wide parallel white racing stripes running lengthwise from the front of the hood to the back bumper. Other than the crush Mr. Prine had developed for Miss Quincy, our young and bookish-looking French Teacher, his MGB Rally Car was the one true love of his life.

We had an old, partially dismantled Pontiac sedan permanently stationed in the garage area of the Shop which was the car we worked on for real and learned how to do basic automotive mechanical tasks during Auto Shop. On this day Mr. Prine was explaining how the electricity from the Coil went through the Distributor, and then traveled from the Rotor out to each Spark Plug. The hood of the Pontiac was propped open, and we were all gathered around it peering into the engine compartment. It was actually a nice moment where all hostilities seemed to have been set aside, as if Jack had decided upon a Truce.

Also, it had snowed heavily for a couple of hours in the late morning leaving a covering of about four inches of fluffy white snow everywhere so everyone was cheerful and excited. We knew we would be throwing a lot of snowballs at recess and that a lot more after-school wintery fun was in store. But, we soon discovered that Jack's softer attitude towards Mr. Prine was, alas, merely a cruel manipulation of Mr. Prine's latent wish for a better relationship with him. His earlier declaration that Mr. Prine was, "no fun", was the equivalent of a death sentence, at least in terms of being useful to our education. I feared the worst for poor Mr. Prine.

Since we were looking at the car's electrical system and its related components, the car's ignition was turned off, but the battery cables were still connected to the battery terminals, and the key was still in the ignition cylinder. Jack politely asked Mr. Prine if we could turn the ignition key on in order to see how the Rotor sent the sparks through the Distributor to the Spark Plugs in real time. He loved cars and engines so his enthusiasm seemed and sounded genuine. Mr. Prine agreed to his request so Jack reached through the driver's side window with his right hand and turned the key on. He winked at me and motioned with his head for us all to stand back. Obediently, we all took a few steps back from the open engine compartment. Then, keeping his long arm through the window and his hand resting on the car's steering wheel, Jack stuck his head forward into the engine compartment as best he could and in an enthusiastic tone asked,

"Hey, Mr. Prine? What's going on over here by the horn?"

With his left hand he was pointing to the car's horn which was mounted near the headlight housing inside the engine compartment. Mr. Prine leaned into the engine compartment to look at what Jack was pointing at, and the second his head got near the horn, Jack pressed down on the middle of the steering wheel with his right hand, and the old Pontiac's horn blared out violently,

"Beeeeeeeep!!! Blaaaaaaaaat!!! Beeeeeeeeep!!!"

Now remember, cars made back then actually had trumpet shaped horns about 6 inches long, two of them side by side, in fact. They looked just like little trumpets, like the blue ones on the top of hand held Air Horns used by fans at Football games and for signaling time-outs at Soccer games. And they were *very, very loud*. When Jack's right hand pressed down on the steering wheel, Mr. Prine's head was only inches away from the car's horns. It was deafeningly loud, and it even hurt my ears standing back about eight feet away from the engine compartment.

Startled by the volume and harshness of the sound, Mr. Prine instinctively jerked his head back out of the engine compartment, away from the sound source. He instantly whacked the back of his head on the underside of the hood, and he hit it pretty hard. His head made a loud clanking noise against the heavy sheet steel of the car's hood. He was kind of stunned by the blow, and we all tried not to laugh, but we didn't succeed. He had walked right into Jack's car horn ambush with both eyes open, it was better than watching the Three Stooges.

Mr. Prine was holding the back of his head with both hands and wincing in pain with both eyes closed. He slowly opened his eyes and stared at Jack who had that blank detached look on his face again. Mr. Prine's gaze drifted to the windows and the snow outside that covered everything thickly. He returned his gaze to Jack and his eyes focused again, still grimacing in pain. Then he said, in a slow and menacing tone,

"McCormack... you... are... going... to... *shovel the entire driveway*... all by yourself... so that Mr. Chandler and I won't have to do it when school ends for the day. In the *meantime*... I will pay a visit to Mr. Fascinelli and explain your little *caper* here today... and I assure you that I will have a nice little *Pink Slip* waiting for you when you finish shoveling... and then you will *report* to Mr. Fascinelli's office. Get your coat on. *Now!*"

We all thought this was pretty harsh punishment. The driveway which led from the street into the Shop entrance at the back of the school was at least sixty feet long and about ten feet wide. Mr. Chandler's 1957 Chevy Station Wagon and Mr. Prine's cherished MGB Rally Car were parked out there hidden just behind the corner of the building. Both cars were out of sight but covered in snow no doubt. It would take Jack at least an hour to do it alone, and he would get his boots soaking wet from the deep snow, and it was cold and windy too. But instead of arguing or begging to be let off, he meekly went to get his coat and seemed genuinely remorseful. Mr. Prine handed him the Shop's snow shovel, and Jack trudged out through the Shop's back door into the wintery weather without a word of protest.

We all went to our next class in a somber mood. I was worried about Jack being out there in the cold, shoveling all that snow by himself. About an hour after he had been sent out there, I caught a glimpse of him from an upstairs window. He was nearly finished with the entire driveway and had done a surprisingly meticulous job. He was still shoveling tirelessly, but instead of throwing the snow off to the side of the driveway as he went along, he was carrying each fluffy shovel-full around the corner of the building and then returning with his empty shovel for another scoop. I was mystified. He had a strangely serene and happy look on his face, almost like the look of someone who has finally achieved a lifelong dream or a significant milestone of some sort. Eventually the entire driveway was shoveled perfectly, every bit of snow was gone, but I wondered where Jack had put it, and why?

I decided to go down to the Shop and see if he was ok. I ran down the stairs and walked into the Shop just as Jack came in from shoveling the snow. He stomped the snow off of his big work boots and returned the shovel to its hook by the door. He seemed subdued and oddly resigned to his fate. He beat his hands against his coat and said,

"Phew, it's pretty cold out there, my hands are freezing! Hey, Mr. Prine, I'm going to Mr. Fascinelli's office now, sorry about the car horn, I really am *really* sorry. I hope you like how good a job I did with the snow on the driveway. Drive home safe, please."

Mr. Prine held out a Pink Slip and pointed towards the door. He said,

"Just get out of here McCormack, just *go*. Mr. Fascinelli *knows* you're coming. I already went to see him, and he *knows exactly* what you did. I'm leaving early, my head *hurts*, thanks to you. Enjoy your *suspension.*"

Then he put on his coat and started out the Shop's back door towards his car. Jack motioned for me to come with him. He walked quickly down the hall and started up the steps, motioning for me to hurry. He grabbed my arm and spoke quickly,

"C'mon, *run*, we have to hurry, I have to get to Fascinelli's office right *away*!"

I didn't know what he was talking about, but I started running and hurrying along just as he had asked. We ran up the stairwell that led onto the first floor, ran down the hall right past our Homeroom, and right into the little waiting room outside of Mr. Fascinelli's office. His receptionist looked up from her desk and said,

"Go in, Jack, he's expecting you."

Jack turned to me and said,

"Thanks for coming with me, I'll see you next week... maybe."

I was mystified as to why his Suspension would be for longer than a day or two. All he had done was to blow the car's horn and cause Mr. Prine to smack his head on the underside of the hood. And he had served his punishment by shoveling the back driveway as told. I left Jack in Mr. Fascinelli's office and turned down the hall back towards our Homeroom. That's when I heard someone running up the stairwell from the Shop area at what sounded like top speed. The footsteps echoed down the long first floor corridor, bouncing off of the shiny floors and the metal lockers lined up down each side. Before I could begin to wonder who would be in such a hurry, the door from the stairway burst open, and I saw that it was Mr. Prine. His coat was unbuttoned, his hair was all sticking up, and he had a wild look on his face.

Parts of his clothes were soaking wet, clumps of snow were clinging to his coat sleeves, and his hands were noticeably bright red. He looked wild and deranged like a crazy person on the loose. He looked like he had become completely unhinged. He was having trouble speaking, but his words were clear to me. In a low strangled voice he asked,

"*Where is he??!! Where is McCormack??!! My car!! My Car!!!*"

He walked right to Mrs. Tromler's room and threw open the door to our Homeroom without knocking. He stood there in the doorway, melting snow dripping from him, and repeated his question to the shocked and silent room. He was breathing hard and gasping for air all at the same time. I remember that the lower halves of the fronts of his pants from the knees down were soaking wet and the sleeves of his coat were soaked too. The Homeroom kids were stunned. Everyone, including Mrs. Tromler, was staring at him, mouths open, unable to respond. Melting snow was making little puddles around his feet on the classroom floor. He kept repeating his question in a detached and faraway voice, as if all of his energy had just been drained from him.

"*Where* is he...? *Where* is he...? *Where's McCormack*...? My *car*... My *car*....

I stepped close to him and told him, in a calm, soothing tone,

"Mr. Prine... Jack's down the hall in Mr. Fascinelli's office just like you wanted. He's not here."

Mr. Prine stared blankly at me as if he couldn't understand what I was saying. I thought maybe the impact of his head against the hood of the Pontiac had been more severe than it had seemed. He blurted out in the same disconnected, almost sobbing voice,

"My *car*... that *kid*... he *buried* my car... it's under a *mountain* of snow... *buried it... buried... mountain of snow... my car...*"

I had never seen an adult, not to mention a teacher, so completely unstrung before. Without thinking about what I was doing, I put my arm around his shoulder and turned him back towards the hallway, gently propelling him and guiding him down the hall. I kept using the same calm and soothing tones,

"It's ok Mr. Prine, I'm sure Mr. Fascinelli can help you... just keep walking down the hall to his office, ok?, Mr. Fascinelli will help you, ok?"

He turned slowly with me and began walking towards Mr. Fascinelli's office. He was mumbling indistinctly, and melted snow was dipping off of him at every step. He looked like a Zombie version of himself. I walked quickly back into our Homeroom, closed the door behind me and went right to my seat. I sat there silently, torn between complete awe at Jack's masterful manipulation of the punishment Mr. Prine had handed out to him, and the shock at seeing the punishment he in turn had actually handed out to poor Mr. Prine. It was a sobering experience. Once again I had encountered an adult who turned out to be painfully child-like and not at all like what I thought an adult should be. It was a recurrent theme in my life without a doubt.

The mystery had been solved as to where Jack had put all of the snow that he had carefully shoveled off of the driveway. Everyone at school soon found out how he had manipulated Mr. Prine and defeated him, and everyone agreed he had achieved his greatest victory to date. Over the next few days the entire story with all the details came to light. Jack never let a punishment go unpunished, as we always said, but this time he had proven his point with a creative display of well aimed revenge. He had punished Mr. Prine by targeting the one thing dearest to him, his MGB Rally Car. Jack had deliberately, diligently, and meticulously shoveled and scraped every bit of snow off of the back driveway, and then he had placed it carefully on top of Mr. Prine's cherished MGB Rally Car, every single shovel full.

Although the car hadn't received even one scratch, it turned out that Jack had done more than just pile all of the snow on top of it. He had taken it to a higher level and created a giant car-shaped snow sculpture which held Mr. Prine's MGB Rally Car captive beneath it. He had taken care to pat it down gently with the shovel and had even gone so far as to sculpt pseudo-tires, a windshield, and headlights. I really wished Mr. Prine had taken a picture of it before he had gone nuts and tried to free the car from all that snow with his hands and arms. I guess he hadn't found Jack's artistic vision quite as fascinating as we all had. That was why he was soaking wet and dripping when he had come upstairs, he hadn't wanted to risk damaging the car by using a snow shovel to free it from under the pile.

Mr. Prine didn't come to school for a whole week after Jack buried his car in the giant snow-car sculpture and neither did Jack. He was suspended for the entire week and placed on a Zero Tolerance Probationary status by Mr. Fascinelli. Mr. Fascinelli told him he would be expelled and remanded to our local Vocational School if he transgressed again. Jack knew that Mr. Fascinelli meant what he said. It was not an idle threat. We were dutifully shocked by this situation and recognized that we would all have to be on our best behavior for a very long time to avoid Mr. Fascinelli's scrutiny.

Mr. Prine arrived at school on the first day back from his "vacation" in a different car, a basic second hand Oldsmobile. His much loved MGB Rally Car would no longer be at risk as a possible target for Jack's schemes. For the rest of the year Mr. Chandler taught our shop class, not Mr. Prine, and Jack reluctantly but wisely let go of his purposeful baiting and tormenting of our teachers. He did not want to go to Vocational School. We would all be going to our town's High School the following September with all of its attendant activities, inter scholastic sports, and social attractions, and Jack did not want to be left out. So things calmed down in a big way at school, and we all fell into the very predictable normal lives of suburban teenagers in good old fashioned middle class America. It was boring, but it was peaceful too.

But before I could go to High School, I would be going away for my first full summer at Riding Camp in Pennsylvania. My Mom had already arranged it as a reward for my supposedly mature and responsible actions of the previous summer. All of the hard earned experiences I had encountered during my childhood and early adolescence would prove to have been good training, sort of, for what I would discover at camp. I didn't know that at Riding Camp I was going to have the most fun you can ever have. I didn't know that my experiences up to that point would seem tame by comparison. I had no idea just what all of that was going to mean in my life, but I had a seriously wonderful time finding out.

Chapter 10

The Midnight Ride Of The Scary Old Cowboy Guy On His Wild Horse

U P UNTIL THE SUMMER BETWEEN my 8th and 9th grade school years my experiences with horses had been limited to what I had read in books or seen on TV, and from having gone on a few trail rides at a local dude ranch. Now, in late June, I found myself at Riding Camp in rural northeastern Pennsylvania for eight whole weeks. I was living in a cabin with a counselor and three other campers, and my entire day was structured around horses and riding. I was a member of the Horsemen by camp definition, the coolest guys at camp, and I loved every minute of it. The only potential glitch was my ongoing tendency to seek out the highest risk situations and engage in them willfully just to see just how far it could all go. In other words, my environment had changed, but I hadn't.

While it offered standard activities like swimming, canoeing, and archery, the heart and soul of the camp was the Riding Program, and the heart and soul of the Riding Program were the Horsemen. The camp maintained a herd of about 50 well schooled horses and ponies, and all of the campers rode in lessons every day. The Riding Staff and the Horsemen made this all possible. Each Horseman was in charge of his own horse for the entire summer, and we learned how to feed, groom, and care for our horses in a practical and sensible manner. We were taught how to clean and maintain the saddle, the bridle, the halter, and the rest of the tack. We learned barn management skills, rode in two or more riding lessons each day, and helped the younger campers learn the basics. Along with all of that, we competed in local horse shows, rode out on group overnight camping trips, and went on long rides along the seemingly endless country roads and out into the many fields that surrounded the camp property. It was like a boy's version of Nirvana for me, or a Viking boy's version of Valhalla with horses thrown in for good measure, as I liked to say.

The absolute most fun and excitement we had at camp was when we played various field games on horseback which usually involved all of the Horsemen on our horses and ponies at the same time. These games would never be allowed nowadays. They would be a liability insurance company's nightmare. The games were exciting, awesomely fun, and at some point they always became more or less out of control. We didn't wear helmets back then, yet no one seemed to ever get seriously injured either. We played three games in particular that were my favorites: Cross The Delaware, The Civil War, and The Cavalry Charge. I doubt my parents would have sent me to the camp if they'd known what we actually did there. Although, to be perfectly honest, the things we did without the horses were even crazier, but I digress.

The main camp complex was at the top of a hill with wide open views of the surrounding countryside. Our Horsemen cabins were arranged on the central Senior Camp Clearing which was a large rectangular open grassy area about two hundred yards long and about one hundred and fifty yards wide. The Senior cabins were on the perimeter of the Clearing with our Horsemen's cabins lined up in a row on one side of it. Right behind our cabins was Old Parsons Road. We had to cross over Old Parsons to get to the riding rings, and we walked up and down it several times a day to the stables, paddocks, and pastures which were located at the bottom of the hill. It was a typical single lane dirt and gravel farm road that connected the rural surrounding farmland with the main blacktop road that led to the nearest town. The town was more like a village or a mini-hamlet. It had one restaurant which was also the only bar in town, and that same business was the only gas station too. The local farmers would go past the camp on their tractors and farm vehicles once in a while, and there was the occasional car or pick up truck, but Old Parsons road was pretty much unused during most days so it was perfect for us and the horses.

Old Parsons Road was a real problem for me. Each summer we would be regaled many times with "The Legend Of Old Parsons Road", a story that was exactly the kind of thing I have always been afraid of. According to the legend, an innocent man had been wrongly convicted of a murder and hung for it sometime in the 1800's. The murder had taken place along Old Parsons Road not far from camp in a swampy area known as The Gully. On the anniversary of his execution, every mid-summer, starting at sunset, the innocent man's restless ghost would walk that section of the road until daybreak in revenge for being wronged.

So on Old Parsons Night, right after sunset, each of us had to walk along the road, alone, in the dark, from the barn area all the way over the hill past our cabins, and then down through the dreaded Gully. Our Counselors would lurk in the underbrush along the roadside making vague scary sounds, and usually one of them would haunt The Gully dressed in shredded clothing wearing a noose around his neck. I just simply hated the whole spectacle which struck me with mortal fear, and I lived in suppressed anxiety about Old Parsons Night each summer. The Counselors would Disqualify you if you hummed, whispered, talked, veered off of the center of the road, or got too close to another camper during your attempt to walk the whole way through The Gully to the finish area. They would write a "D", for "Disqualified", on your forehead with a magic marker, and the next day everyone else would know you had chickened out or failed the test. I never even tried to make it past our cabins because the whole thing was just too much for my delicate suburban psyche. I avoided scary movies and stories like the plague in case you're wondering.

The Counselors told us other spooky stories about various semi-mythical creatures and characters that populated the area, but who only came out at night. One of my favorite Counselors warned me not to cross Old Parsons to get to the lavatory and shower house at night because giant predatory *Squirrels* lurked in the woods nearby just waiting for fresh victims to fall into their paws. To be honest, I still glance over my shoulder when I walk from our garage to our house at night because of that story, never mind going down into the basement.

When the Counselors told us these unsettling tales, they always made a point of warning us that at night things could get a bit weird. This was due to the unpredictable appearances of The Purple Taxi, The Pink Helicopter, The Haunted House Boys, and the sporadic social agenda of The Scary Old Cowboy

Guy On His Wild Horse. We all thought that these were obvious fakes devised to keep us indoors at night, but as I found out all too soon, one of these figures was really, really, *real.*

About two weeks into my first month at camp I was sleeping peacefully in my bunk, dreaming that I was galloping a horse along a country road at top speed. In my dream I could hear my horse's hoof beats echoing off of the hard surface of the road... and then something woke me up. It was about 3 AM or thereabouts. My counselor and my bunkmates were sleeping like logs. The usual sounds of the night were filtering through the open windows of our cabin. My sleepiness began to dissolve when I thought I heard a far off shout and then the barest hint of a horse galloping in the distance. I was still in a half-dream state and couldn't tell if it was real or not. I sat up thinking maybe it was only an owl hooting or a dog barking, or some unidentifiable alien creepy forest creature that my too vivid imagination was inventing, but it wasn't. The distinct sound of a horse galloping on the hard gravelly surface of Old Parsons Road was now unmistakably real. A shiver went right through me in spite of the warmth of the summer night.

Then I heard a second definitely non-fictitious sound, another garbled shout far off in the night. My heart began to race. I looked around and saw that my cabin mates were still sound asleep. I now had no doubt that a horse was galloping towards camp from somewhere off in the distance, and that someone or *something* was riding it. Visions of the Headless Horseman arose before me. I began to sweat a bit. I lay back down and pulled the covers over my head, but my curiosity got the better of me, so I sat up again.

I don't know what compelled me to do it, but I got out of my bunk, wrapped my blanket around my shoulders, and crept out the door of our cabin. I inched my way around to the back of it right near the road. I crouched down behind a big tree next to Old Parsons and carefully peeked around it. I'm sure I was holding my breath. Was this for real? Why wasn't I back in the cabin safe among my bunkmates? I was mortally afraid of the road itself, and I have always been afraid of the dark, but my desire to see whatever was out on the road that night was overpowering. The clattering of the hooves was coming on fast, and a man's voice was plainly audible amid the sounds of scattering gravel and the heavy breathing of a horse running flat out. I was frozen with a strange fascination that was mixed with excitement and fear. And then I caught sight of them as they came into full view, galloping at breakneck speed towards me in the eerie shadows cast across the road by the flat white moonlight.

This was no phantom apparition. This was a very real, very muscular looking, dun colored horse, lathered and sweating, nostrils flaring, mane and tail streaming out, galloping straight down Old Parsons Road. The reins were flying loose, and sparks were shooting off of its hooves where they were hitting the hardened road surface. It may have been about 15 or 16 hands high, but it was hard to tell. The horse's body was low to the ground, and it was going totally flat out, coming from the direction of town. The shadows of the trees that were cast across the road by the moonlight created a strobe effect as the horse moved from light to dark and light to dark every split second. It came thundering past me so fast as I huddled behind my tree that I barely had time to really see it. As the horse roared by I got an unimpeded full-on view of its rider. He was an older man, swaying dangerously from side to side in a big old western saddle with a battered cowboy hat trailing behind him like a drag racer's parachute. In the moment that he went flying past me I swear it looked like he had only one good eye, and then they disappeared around the bend in the road and were gone. They were swallowed up by the darkness, and the sound of their mad galloping receded gradually until the night was silent and still again.

I was stunned, frozen in place by the surreal images and feelings of the moment. No one else was awake in the entire camp but me. Even the crickets had stopped their incessant chirping for a few moments. I sank to the ground and pulled my blanket close around me as my breathing gradually returned to normal and the sounds of the night returned. Eventually, I crept back into the cabin and slipped into my bunk. I lay there for a long time staring out the open window towards Old Parsons Road, replaying the incredible scene in my mind again and again. I wanted to understand what I had witnessed. I needed some kind of an explanation, because now I *knew* that this particular myth was for real, and it had touched something very deep within me.

The next day I asked one of my Counselors if he knew anyone who had ever seen The Scary Old Cowboy Guy On His Wild Horse. He said that if anyone had actually ever seen them they had kept it to themselves. He said everyone knew about the two of them, but no one ever spoke about them because no one really thought it was a true story. I asked him to give me any information he had. He explained that the Old Cowboy Guy was supposedly a farmer who lived a few miles farther along Old Parsons Road from camp. On occasional weekend evenings he would ride the dun colored horse into town, tie it to the hitching post in front of the restaurant-bar-gas station, treat himself to dinner and then drink himself silly late into the night. Generally, sometime after midnight, the farmer would stagger out of the bar, mount the horse and turn its head towards home. The horse knew the drill and would carry the old man home, galloping flat out all the way back to the farm. This system enabled the farmer to avoid the potential problems of driving home at night under the influence of alcohol. The counselor added that he had never actually seen this for himself, and believed that it was more myth than reality. In his opinion it was a scary campfire tale told to the campers to keep them from leaving their cabins at night. But there was more to the story.

I got the rest of the story from one of the other local farmers who delivered our hay and oats. The full legend of the dun colored horse was that it was a wild mustang the farmer had tracked and followed alone for ten days through the mountains and countryside a number of years ago. He had finally cornered it and broken it to ride, but the horse had never been truly tamed. The wild moonlit scene I had witnessed that night was sort of an agreement between the farmer and the formerly wild horse, as far as I could understand. In exchange for being controlled by the farmer most of the time, the dun colored mustang would purposefully be allowed to go galloping off into the night every other week or two, thereby staying in touch with its true wild self.

I decided to keep my strange and exhilarating night sighting a secret which ranks as one of the only secrets I ever kept completely under wraps in my entire life. But it became my personal dream to gallop on an uncontrolled horse, flat out down a country road, throwing caution to the wind, released from the everyday constraints of my middle class suburban life. Somehow, my favorite Counselor must have known this idea had formed in my mind, because at the end of that first fateful summer he gave me a strange poster-sized print he had found in an antique shop somewhere. It was an unusual abstract painting of a dappled gray horse with purple wings running across the sky against a huge red sun with these words splashed across the lower section:

"Whatever else you leave Undone, just once ride a Wild Horse into the Sun."

I put that quote beneath my high school graduation photograph three years later, but no one really understood what it meant except me. However, when I came back to camp for my second summer ten months later, the Wild Horse of my dreams also arrived during the first week from a dealer out west. Once again, my life had taken a turn that influenced me forever, but I didn't know it yet. I didn't know that I was going to become a younger version of The Scary Old Cowboy Guy On His Wild Horse, and I didn't know that nothing would ever be the same for me again.

Chapter 11

Would You Like To See Where The Horse Bit Me?

HIS NAME WAS BIG RED, which made no sense at all because he wasn't really that big, and he wasn't really red. He was more like a mottled pinkish brown which is a kindhearted description of his uniquely unattractive coloring. He was about seven years old or so, and when they took him off of the horse van, having come all the way from Arizona, we all agreed that he was the ugliest horse we'd ever seen. Technically he was what's called a Strawberry Roan, but that didn't even come close to an accurate description. He looked like a light gray horse that someone had splashed all over with buckets of dark purple and brown paint. There were big mottled splotches of this coloring on his neck and shoulders, and clusters of little flecks on his head, but the flecks were half brownish purple and half grayish brown.

His physique was more like that of a plow horse than anything else. He was only about 15 hands high, powerfully muscular, broad chested, and he had big round hooves. He had a roached mane which means it had been buzzed off with clippers like a crew-cut, but it had grown out about four inches so he looked kind of like a Roman horse. He was dejected looking and dirty, but he was built like an off-road military vehicle, and looked like he had some potential. He gave the impression that he could run through a stone wall which, as it turned out later that summer, he almost did, with me along for the ride. He had a gentle and patient look on his tired face, and I felt drawn to him in a strangely sympathetic way.

There were five of us who were Counselors In Training, or C.I.T.s, at camp that year, and we were a close knit group. We were all about the same age and had similar temperaments. We shared a quirky sense of humor and a tendency to look for rules that needed bending. There was Casey, our unofficial leader, the son of a prominent lawyer; Carter, a well-bred Virginian; Gino, born and raised in The Bronx; Toby, another lawyer's son; and Me. We worked full time with the horses, taught lessons to the younger campers throughout the day, and had other responsibilities in our respective cabins.

Ranked immediately above the five of us were the four Riding Instructors, the "R.I.s", who were basically our Superior Officers. We called them, "The

Flunkies." At the top of this chain of command was the Head Riding Instructor, the Major General of the program, who we all called the "H.R.I." The H.R.I. and the Riding Instructors were college aged guys who had had been at the camp since they were little kids. The C.I.T.s were similar to them in that way because, except for me, everyone else had been coming to the camp since they were eight or nine years old. So, within the framework of our busy day to day schedule, we naturally spent our free time cooking up ways to make the Instructors lives miserable, and we were very, very good at that.

On the day Big Red arrived we all walked around and looked at him, felt his legs, and checked out his teeth. Then we trotted him out. When he went from walking to trotting out, he immediately transformed, coming up into an unexpectedly athletic frame that showed balance and coordination. His muscular power and latent strength appeared as if by magic. He still had that gentle and patient expression in his huge brownish-yellow eyes, but there was an underlying spark and spirit that twinkled in them too. After we gave him a bath his coat didn't look so bad after all, and I kind of thought he looked like my kind of horse. I secretly cherished the hope that they would assign him to me, but the Head Riding Instructor claimed him for himself. I was crushed, but kept that fact hidden.

The horse assigned to me for that summer was an elegant, golden amber colored gelding named Morning Squire who had an unpredictable nature and a highly developed mean streak. He often behaved as if he bore a grudge against the Universe for forcing him be a horse when he should have been a duke, or a prince, or some kind of corporate executive. He was about 16.1 hands high so he was a tall and athletic looking horse who definitely had my number. He knew I was afraid of him, which I was, and for good reason too.

The prior summer I had been grooming my horse in the stall next to Morning Squire's stall, foolishly oblivious to Squire's intolerance of humans. I was busily curry combing away, pausing every few strokes to remove the accumulated hair and dirt off of the curry comb by knocking it against the partition wall that separated me from Squire. Apparently this constant knocking noise aggravated him. Before I knew what was happening, he reached over the partition, clamped his teeth onto my left shoulder blade and lifted me off the floor for a moment before my t-shirt and some skin gave way, and down I went. It was really a shock and really painful. For the rest of my life I've had a wicked fear of turning my back on any horse in a stall. When I am tanned in the summer, you can still see two perfectly defined tooth-shaped scars that are the visible reminder of Morning Squire's hair-trigger temper.

I got bitten in the back of the head by a thoroughbred stallion later in my career, but that was a one-time chance encounter. Morning Squire and I had to spend a lot of time together early in my second season at camp, and I always had to be on my guard with him. So I wasn't really happy about being Morning Squire's Horseman as you can well imagine. We had a truce of sorts, but he was always giving me the hairy eyeball, and I was very uncomfortable being in a stall with him. But he was wonderful to ride, very athletic, and he couldn't bite me when I was on his back although at times he made it plain that he was thinking about it.

The Riding Instructors were very taken with the British rock band, The Who, that summer, so they renamed the new horse Whiskey Man after their song, *Whiskey Man My Friend.* Years later I wrote and recorded a country western styled song titled, "My Friend Whiskey", in honor of the horse and that song by the Who. It's always a favorite with audiences. The name suited the new horse well, but he was not destined to be the H.R.I.'s horse for long.

Whiskey Man had been trained, or *not* trained as the case may be, to be ridden Western style so he was accustomed to Western bits with long shanks that gave his rider enormous controlling leverage. He literally had callouses in the corners of his mouth where the bit made contact, and this gave him a well developed lack of sensitivity and a willingness to pull hard against the reins and any attempts to control him. He was also accustomed to big heavy Western saddles which enabled his riders to be much more secure on his back than in the English style saddles we used. We rode English style, the same way Cavalry horses were ridden all over the world. So the H.R.I put a nice gentle egg-butt snaffle bit on Whiskey Man's bridle and assumed he could manage the horse. He was a very experienced rider, and he was a big strong guy too. It didn't take very long to find out that he was very, very wrong.

It quickly became apparent that he might as well have just ridden Whiskey Man without a bridle or reins. The horse was more or less untrained, didn't know how to jump, and he was what we called a "dead runaway". That meant that once he got up to speed he would show no inclination whatsoever of slowing down or obeying the commands of his rider. Once he got his engines fired up the best you could hope for was some generalized steering, a minimum of control which enabled the rider to execute gradual semi-circular turning maneuvers that would eventually slow the horse down, but of course the rider still had to be in the saddle to accomplish that.

Whiskey Man's tendency to gallop off into the Wild Blue Yonder with his rider clinging helplessly aboard was revealed in spectacular style on our very first trail ride about a week after he arrived at camp. It was a "No Camper" trail ride on an otherwise quiet evening in June. We left the barnyard and stables and headed up Old Parsons Road back past our Horsemen Cabins. It was only the H.R.I, the Instructors, and the five of us Counselors In Training. The Instructors rode in a group up front just behind the H.R.I, and all of them were being purposefully casual and debonair. We, the lowly C.I.Ts, rode in our own group together about fifty feet behind them awaiting the inevitable signal to trot, or canter, or hopefully to turn off into one of the enormous hayfields bordering the road in anticipation of some real fun. We looked like one of those Civil War paintings of Robert E. Lee trotting along some fence-lined road in Virginia on his way to another victory, surrounded by his famous generals with a small clump of Aides-de-Camp respectfully tagging along.

We pictured ourselves this way mostly due to our obsession with The Civil War Game, one of the more complicated mounted field games we played every summer. During The Civil War Game, normal camp activities were suspended. The entire body of campers and staff were divided up into North vs South, and we got to be The Cavalry while everyone else had to be The Infantry. We would then conduct a campaign for three crazy days, running amuck all over the general camp vicinity trying to capture one another and launching full out Cavalry Charges every chance we got. I don't know how many times I fell off of my horse during The Civil War Game, but thank goodness the fields and paths were relatively soft.

So on Whiskey Man's first extended trail ride the Head Riding Instructor gave us the eagerly awaited signal with a wave his hand and led us at a trot up into one of the big open fields. Upon his next command we fanned out into a classic cavalry battle line formation. We had ten horses in the line, kind of like a chorus line of dancers in a musical, but without the skimpy outfits or the feathered headpieces. Whiskey Man and the H.R.I. were in the center of the line, and it looked like it was going to be business as usual. Up to that point the horse had seemed docile and responsive to the slightest pressures on the reins, and he seemed to move off the H.R.I.'s leg with no resistance at all. So the H.R.I. took it up a notch or two, and we followed suit trotting briskly along still maintaining a nicely formed line.

The H.R.I gave us the signal to shift up to a faster gait, and we broke into a slow relaxed canter. Whiskey Man lowered his head and flexed his awesomely powerful neck in against the controlling influences of the bit and reins. In response, the H.R.I. braced his upper body against the reins, pulling back firmly to control the horse. Whiskey Man countered this by surging ahead of the other horses by a stride or two, his neck still bowed. The more the H.R.I. pulled back, the more the horse resisted, and his pace increased from a canter to a steady slow gallop. Things began to change rapidly.

Please remember that we did not wear helmets back then. I pity today's riders who never get to feel their hair blowing straight back in the breeze created when you are galloping a horse flat out for no reason whatsoever across endless open fields. In the span of about twenty strides all ten horses were galloping in an impromptu race over the broad expanse of the field. It was awesome for us, but for Whiskey Man it was a chance to do the only thing he was really good at... galloping at top speed in a straight line towards an endless horizon, and he was taking the H.R.I. along for the ride whether he liked it or not.

For some reason Whiskey Man had failed to pick up on the Robert E. Lee vibe. Maybe he never saw any of those old prints or paintings. Maybe he didn't pay attention in school when they were studying the Civil War. Regardless of his lack of education he was beginning to drive forward with his haunches under him, balanced and fluid, displaying an unexpected beautifully rhythmic athleticism. The docile plow horse had disappeared, and Whiskey Man's true nature revealed itself. His head came up, his ears were forward, and the look in his eye was full of spark and energy. He was on a mission to shed the Robert E. Lee vibe and to look more like that photograph of Secretariat winning the Kentucky Derby several lengths ahead of the field. But there was no discernible finish line at the end of this race other than the far horizons.

It was breathtaking. It was beautiful. It was unbelievable, and of course we all thought it was incredibly funny too. The whole situation got more and more out of control very quickly. Whiskey Man just wanted to run, and he clearly wanted to be running out in front of the other horses no matter what it took. First, he was one length ahead, then two lengths, and the more the rest of us urged our horses forward to achieve more speed, the faster he went, and the distance between us grew. Clods of turf and bits of gravel were flying back off of his hind feet as he dug into the ground to propel himself forward. The H.R.I. had ceased to be in charge. He had become an unwilling passenger on a powerful undisciplined horse running flat out, pedal to the floor, with no end in sight. The H.R.I.'s useless efforts to haul on the reins were comedic. He was standing up in the stirrups, trying to use his body leverage to influence Whiskey Man, but Whiskey Man wasn't buying it. The rest of us were trailing along farther and farther behind and loving every minute of it.

So off into the Wild Blue Yonder they went, having by now left us far behind. At the end of the field that we were galloping across was a curving lane connecting to another big hay field beyond it. The two of them rocketed into the lane and disappeared behind the trees. The last we saw of them, the H.R.I.

was still standing straight up in the stirrups, yanking and pulling on the reins, and yelling,

"Whoa!! Darn It!! Whoa!! Whoa!!!

Of course we all found this to be unbelievably funny, and we mimicked it unmercifully for the rest of the summer. From that day forth every time anyone's horse showed the least sign of forward movement, or any movement whatsoever, one of us would call out the fateful phrase,

"Whoa!! Darn It!! Whoa!! Whoa!!!

Our collective ongoing mockery of the H.R.I. ended up creating a powerful animosity between our little brotherhood of C.I.T.s and our prideful General Commander. More on that later.

It turned out that the only thing Whiskey Man didn't like to run into or through were dense clumps of trees. This was very important information because on our regular trail rides and overnight camping trips it was the only way to get him to stop galloping once he got up a good head of steam. He had one other problem which we had seen in action. He went from zero to sixty in a surprisingly short time for a horse of his stocky build. He was what Thoroughbred Racing folks would call a "sprinter", but he had "bottom" too, which meant he was gifted with stamina and endurance. So he didn't jump much, he wasn't elegant or responsive, he looked out of place in a Horse Show arena, but *man* could he run, and run he did, every chance he got.

The day after Whiskey Man took the H.R.I. away on that first famous thrill ride, I heard from Casey that the H.R.I. had contacted the dealer and told have him to come and take Whiskey Man back. Furthermore, he had told the dealer that the horse was useless for our program and basically unrideable. I couldn't believe what I had heard. It was the first time in my life I had ever felt a connection with another living creature other than my beloved family dog, Dusty. I was determined to save Whiskey Man from the uncertainties that awaited him if he were sent back to the dealer. Although, speaking of my beloved dog, Dusty, she actually bit me in the head once too, a recurrent theme one might say, but I loved her none the less.

I went immediately into the main barn and knocked on the Tack Room door, committed to preventing Whiskey Man from being banished merely because he had made the H.R.I. look bad in front of everyone. I knew in my heart that he was a good horse. I pleaded my case before the H.R.I., and said I would work extra hard to make Whiskey Man useful. I promised him I would train him to be a good riding horse, and told him all I needed was time. He nodded his head a couple of times and said he would think about it.

About an hour after I had boldly asked the H.R.I. to let me have Whiskey Man as my summer project, one of The Flunkies approached me in the barnyard.

I was wondering what I had done wrong this time when he told me it had been decided that I would give Morning Squire to the H.R.I., and the H.R.I. was giving Whiskey Man to me. I couldn't believe my luck. The truth was that I didn't have a lot of formal equitation training, and Morning Squire was more or less being wasted on me, so the Riding Instructors probably figured Whiskey Man and I could learn to be useful together. I didn't care what their reasons were, Whiskey Man had become my horse for the entire summer, or more accurately, I had become his human.

I was a survivalist kind of rider. It's an understatement to say that I did not have a refined equitation style. All I really wanted to do was to ride out on the many nearby dirt farm roads, and I couldn't get enough of riding through the extensive fields surrounding the camp. I fell off fairly often, but I didn't really mind falling off. I saw it as part of staying on so to speak. So Whiskey Man was not sent back to the dealer much to my relief. He became my personal equine rocket ship, my own four legged drag racer, and a willing partner in near disaster. To be perfectly honest it was nothing short of unconditional True Love.

Chapter 12

The Railroad Tie Caper

IN ADDITION TO MY HIGHLY enjoyable day to day work and my extra hours of effort to train Whiskey Man, one of my favorite related activities was helping to build jumps and obstacles out on the Cross Country Course. In fact, years later I ended up building Cross Country Courses professionally for the sport of Horse Trials which is still a very big part of my life. We didn't call it, "Horse Trials", when we were at camp back then, we called it, "The Military Competition". This was because Cavalry officers had always relied upon fast, powerful horses that were obedient, courageous, and athletic, and our camp had been founded upon basic Cavalry principles. We rode on the Flat, jumped Show Jumps in the riding ring, and galloped and jumped over the Cross Country Courses out in the fields.

When the Head Riding Instructor announced that we were going to build a new Drop Jump out of railroad ties, I was eager to get to work. But first we needed to acquire some railroad ties. One evening just before dark, he told us we were going to take the big green flatbed truck down to the Railroad Company Depot where they had piles of old ties that were, "free for the taking." This didn't seem quite right to us, but we accepted his story none the less.

The H.R.I. drove the big green flatbed truck with one of the Flunkies riding up front in the cab with him. We had figured the foreman of the camp's Maintenance Crew would be involved, but he was nowhere to be seen. The five of us had to ride in the back of the flatbed, and the H.R.I. cautioned us not to talk loudly or make any noise. We thought this was strange, and somehow we knew that he was up to something. It was late in the evening and starting to get dark which I thought was also a bit odd too. We rolled slowly down a long one lane dirt track that threaded its way through a lot of fields and patches of woods until it came out into a clearing. In the clearing were big neatly stacked piles of railroad ties, hundreds of them. They were obviously old ones that had been pulled up and replaced, but they would certainly serve our purposes. All they needed was a fresh coat of Creosote, plus they were "free for the taking". The H.R.I. pulled the flatbed to a stop alongside one of the piles. We all jumped down onto the ground and stared at the big heavy timbers. He pointed at the pile and instructed us to begin putting the ties onto the truck. He told us,

"Handle them carefully and try not to make a lot of noise, we don't want to attract attention down here."

The whole thing did not feel right to us. We knew we were definitely being used as pawns in some kind of after-hours shenanigans, but we went to work as told. It took three of us to handle the weight of each of the railroad ties, so Casey, Toby, and I stayed on the ground while Carter and Gino climbed back up onto the flatbed. We handed the timbers up to them, and they stacked them in a long row crossways on the flatbed's deck. The ties weighed a lot, and we had trouble getting them up to Carter and Gino. In maybe fifteen minutes we had about eight of them stacked neatly on the flatbed. It was getting pretty dark by then, and the H.R.I. had turned on the truck's headlights to give us some light to work by. It made for an eerie scene with the three of us struggling to manhandle the heavy timbers in the glaring beams of the truck's headlights while the H.R.I. and the Flunky stood there supervising us. They seemed a bit on edge and kept looking back up the dirt track every few seconds. Things were moving along fairly smoothly, and we thought that maybe our concerns were misplaced. Maybe it was, "Situation Normal", as Han Solo once announced.

Then the Normal Situation changed into being an Abnormal Situation very quickly. Our attention was caught by the sound of a vehicle coming down the dirt track at a pretty good rate of speed. Its headlights were bouncing up and down in the dark night sky as it negotiated the ruts and bumps along the way. As the vehicle approached the depot a red and blue light began spinning on its roof, and we realized it was our local police officer, Constable Tom Mitchell. This did not look good. All of a sudden I got a flashback to when The First Responder Fireman Guy had made his disorganized appearance at the Johnson's house on the day Timmy and I had set fire to the field. I found myself wondering how this was going to unfold for us.

Constable Tom's police car pulled into the depot's yard area and slid to a stop with his headlights shining full on us. He jumped out of his cruiser waving a big flashlight all around. Casey, Toby, and I were in the act of picking up a railroad tie and handing it up to Gino and Carter on the flatbed. Constable Tom pointed his flashlight at us and said, in a commanding tone,

"Put down that timber, boys, put it down right now!"

We hastily put the railroad tie on the ground and stood there feeling very exposed in the glare of the Constable's headlights. He had the big flashlight in his hands and was waving it around in the faces of each of us in turn including the Flunky and the H.R.I.

He was in his Constable's uniform and looked pretty formidable. He turned to the H.R.I. and said,

"What're you boys doin' down here? These here timbers belong to the Railroad! If I didn't know any better, I'd say you were *stealing* these timbers! What's going on?"

He did not look like he was kidding. And after all, he *was* the law in this area and was known to have a no-nonsense approach to his job. In fact he had a reputation for being more commanding than he needed to be in a lot of circumstances. He also had a reputation for not being the brightest bulb on the tree. And that's when my eyes were opened once again to the delicate grasp on reality that most adults actually have. I harkened back again to the disappointing arrival of the First Responder Fireman Guy when the big hay field was on fire, and I was thankful the railroad ties weren't burning.

But the H.R.I. had already figured out how to turn this sticky situation around. He walked up to Constable Tom in a relaxed, unhurried, and soothingly friendly manner, but with an exasperated expression on his face. He pointed towards the timbers up on the flatbed and said in a cheerful tone,

"Howdy Tom, nice summer evening we've got here, hey? Now Tom, don't jump to any conclusions, just hold on a minute, no need to get riled up... You see, we're not *stealing* any timbers, no sir. You see, we didn't need so many of these old timbers up at camp, so I figured we could just run 'em down here and add 'em to the pile. That's why we brought 'em down here on the flatbed. We figured the Railroad wouldn't mind a few more *old timbers* here and there, if you catch my drift..."

He winked at Constable Tom and left his words hanging expectantly in the warm summer air. I couldn't believe he had really said what he had said, but we all had really heard him. Was Officer Tom going to buy such an obvious reversal of the truth?

"...just run 'em down here and add 'em to the pile?"

Was he serious? We were *obviously* stealing the railroad ties. But Officer Tom's brow began to furrow, and a puzzled look came to his face. He had not seen us actually put any railroad ties up onto the truck, and for all he knew Gino and Carter had just handed down the one we'd been hefting when he arrived on the scene. As his expression became more thoughtful, we saw that the H.R.I. had judged his man correctly. He knew Constable Tom was not quick on the uptake, and that he liked giving orders and being in command. The H.R.I. added in a plaintive voice,

"C'mon Tom, give us a break, the Railroad fellas won't notice *twenty or so* old timbers added to these piles... what do you say? Don't make us pick 'em up again, they weigh a ton, and these boys have had a long day."

Officer Tom's brow furrowed even deeper. He looked at the truck. He looked at the H.R.I., and then he looked again to where Toby, Casey and I were still standing by the nearest pile of railroad ties. Clearly the H.R.I. had put his money on Constable Tom's need to be in charge at all times. After a long agonizing silence he shook his head forcefully and delivered his verdict,

"Nope, nope, *can't* do that, just can't allow it, it ain't right. You boys have to put those timbers back up on that truck. You hear? You can't just do whatever you want around here, boys, this is railroad property. It just ain't *right*."

We were staring at each other in disbelief. Was this really happening? Was the H.R.I. about to succeed in getting Officer Tom to actually *command* us to steal the railroad ties? For that was definitely the case. We were here, on railroad property, in the dark, taking "free" timbers for our Drop Jump. But instead of being busted for the obvious theft, we were being ordered to take the ties "*back to camp*", even though they had never been at camp in the first place. Constable Tom asked,

"How many of them timbers did you boys put on the ground so far? I want the truth now, you hear.?"

The H.R.I. said, with a slight catch in his voice,

"Oh, probably fifteen or thereabouts, *isn't that right boys...?*"

We didn't know whether or not to go along with this, but before we could answer Constable Tom pounced on the H.R.I.'s words,

"You said *twenty* timbers just a minute ago! It *was* twenty, I remember you said it! Now... you boys still got eight timbers on the truck, so I'm going to stand *right here* while you pick up those other twelve ties you already dropped off, and I'm going to watch you put 'em back up on there!"

The H.R.I. made sounds of protest, but Constable Tom shut him off with a stern and commanding Police Guy "Halt!" hand signal, holding his arm straight out with his fingers held together pointing upwards, and his palm aimed at the H.R.I.

"I don't want to hear *another* word now. You boys pick up those twelve timbers and get 'em back on that truck and take 'em back to camp, right now!"

The H.R.I. dropped his shoulders in resignation and signaled for us to follow Constable Tom's orders. Under the good Constable's stern commanding stare we dutifully "reloaded" twelve more ties onto the flatbed. The H.R.I. tried to get Constable Tom to reverse his decision one more time, but he got shot down again. Constable Tom meant business. He was a no-nonsense guy. Rules were rules. Regretfully, still shaking his head, the H.R.I. climbed up into the cab of the truck. We all climbed up onto the back with our twenty railroad ties. As the flatbed slowly turned and left the yard area, Constable Tom stood there still watching us warily. After all, rules were rules.

So our suspicions were confirmed. The H.R.I. had used us to steal the railroad ties, at night, right from the Railroad company supply depot. He had deftly manipulated Constable Tom into becoming an accomplice by playing upon his weaknesses and exposing him to be painfully gullible which we felt was mean and arrogant. Granted, the railroad ties we took were old timbers that had been replaced, but it was still pretty sneaky. We were offended by the fact that we had been caught between the H.R.I. and Constable Tom, and had been forced into being unwilling conspirators. We were beginning to see that we would have to defend ourselves from the H.R.I.'s schemes. We also collectively decided that our best Defense would be a good Offense, and a truly good Offense required us to be a little bit *offensive*. We were quite happy to take the steps needed to make that happen. Basically, without anyone really saying it, we declared war on the H.R.I and the Flunkies.

Chapter 13

Blue Gall, Red Gall, and The Alphabet Burp

THE ALL OUT WAR BETWEEN the Riding Instructors and the C.I.Ts became the dominant theme at camp that summer, and it gathered momentum quickly. It's important to understand how close knit a group that we, the younger guys, were. We considered ourselves to be Brothers In Arms, united against the oppression of the H.R.I. and his circle of Flunkies. It was Us against Them, plain and simple.

It all started with us making fun of the H.R.I's vain attempts to control Whiskey Man on that first fateful trail ride. This irritated him to a degree that we found delightful, therefore we made it a staple of our day to day activities. One morning Toby was picking out his horse's hooves which he did first thing each day after bringing the horses in from the pastures. We had old fashioned straight stalls built in rows under open pavilion roofs. The open and airy design of the stables was perfect for summer, but horses could not live in them during the winter. The horses stood in the stalls for grooming, feeding, and tacking up, but otherwise they were in lessons, out on trail rides, or turned out in the huge pastures surrounding the barn area. Toby's horse was a much loved older bay named Flash. He was very calm, patient, well trained, and athletic. As Toby picked up his right forefoot, Flash wiggled his neck to shake off a fly. It was a completely normal and non-aggressive act on his part. Toby jumped back and started calling out,

"Whoa!! Darn It!!, Whoa!!!, *Whoa!!!*"

This was high comedy for us. The horse had barely twitched his neck muscles, but Toby was acting like his life was being threatened by an unruly beast. The rest of us found this to be hysterically funny, and we immediately adopted it as a standard part of our daily routine. Whenever one of the horses moved slightly, took a step forward during a lesson, moved its head to shake off a fly, or just for no reason whatsoever, we would get all panicky-sounding and start repeating the fateful phrase,

"Whoa!! Darn It!!, Whoa!!!, *Whoa!!!*"

The Flunkies hated this with a passion because they knew we were mocking the H.R.I., their all-powerful leader. Needless to say the H.R.I. quickly became aware of our new game, and he put the

Flunkies on alert to squash this affront to his precious dignity. Their attempts to repress us were met with hostility and a generalized lack of respect. Let's be realistic, we were sixteen year old boys, quite full of ourselves, and in the distasteful role of being the oppressed subordinates. We didn't get paid to be C.I.Ts, our parents still paid the full camp fee, but the Instructors, who were only a few years older than us, were all on salary. Plus, we were intelligent, capable, and bound together by our united sense of being low men on the totem pole.

So the H.R.I. called a Staff Meeting in the Tack Room which was in the Main Barn. The Tack Room was the private sanctuary of the Instructors. We weren't allowed in there unless we were invited or given permission, or were called in to be reprimanded or lectured, and we knew this wasn't going to be a pep talk. All of the old-school medications we used back then were kept in the Tack Room. The two mainstays were called Red Gall and Blue Gall, both were old-school Cavalry medications. Red Gall was for wounds or abrasions in areas that needed to stay soft and pliable, like on a leg joint or a cut over a large muscle. Blue Gall was for anything that needed to be dried out, like a bite or cut over the rib cage or on the head. Red Gall was relatively oily, but it could be washed out of cloth or off of skin with detergent. Blue Gall was like ink. Once you got Blue Gall on your fingers or skin it stayed for about two weeks. Blue Gall gave human skin an iridescent shine too.

So we filed into the Tack Room under the baleful glares of the the Flunkies, and waited for the H.R.I. to speak. I noticed that a bottle of Blue Gall was sitting on the counter near his hand. I also noticed that the Flunkies looked smug, as if they couldn't wait to see our reaction to what was coming. The H.R.I. made it short and simple. First off, he referred to the currently popular withering parody of his fruitless attempts to control Whiskey Man on the day of the trail ride. Then in a dark and menacing voice he intoned,

"I know what all of you are doing, and I don't like it. From now on, any C.I.T. who dares to mock me in public, either verbally or by his actions, will be *punished*. He will be tackled by the Riding Instructors, held down, and have his *entire face* painted with Blue Gall. I'm giving you fair warning. And if I find out that you are still doing it behind my back, the punishment will be worse than that."

We were stunned and incredulous. A quick glance at my fellow C.I.T.s confirmed our unified outrage at this heavy handed attempt to stifle our comedic creativity. How dare he take this threatening tone with us? Another glance confirmed my own feelings that we were not going to take this lying down either. No Way. This meant War. It was time to take off the gloves. It was time to show our true colors. It was time to unleash our arsenal of disruptive tactics, and without a doubt we all knew that first on the list would be... The Alphabet Burp. Nothing less would do.

The Alphabet Burp was Toby's unfulfilled Quixotic dream to say the entire alphabet, out loud, in one disgustingly rude continuous burp. He had been working on this insane idea for several summers. It originated with his unquenchable passion for Orange Crush soda which was available at The Canteen, our camp's snack bar. With the rest of us in attendance, Toby would gulp down two or three Orange Crushes, and then his face would take on a weirdly glazed look which we all came to recognize. We'd gather around expectantly, and then he would abruptly blurt out the Alphabet up to whatever letter he was able to reach, but in a low, guttural, absolutely inappropriate voice, kind of like a very rude, very large bullfrog. This performance never failed to just kill us. We loved it, and as the summers rolled by Toby got older and bigger and able to drink more Orange Crush, and then on one memorable July evening he made it the whole way. It was his Magnum Opus, his Holy Grail. We picked him up on our shoulders and paraded him around the camp. We sensed that it was going to play a key role in our hostile relationship with the H.R.I. and the Flunkies.

It just so happened that the H.R.I had a prissy streak as well as an overinflated ego, and he hated burping, spitting, not using napkins, and all of the other of the things that boys find essential to life itself. Consequently he truly *hated* The Alphabet Burp, and therefore we made it our mission to make it part of his life. So one fateful afternoon Casey, our unofficial spokesman, formally requested a meeting with the H.R.I. He told him the purpose of the meeting was that we wanted to, "*Air our Grievances*", as he put it. How Casey *ever* said that without cracking up is a mystery to me.

At the appointed hour we filed into the Tack Room and stood together in a row facing the H.R.I. He had all four of the Flunkies standing with him, and they all had grimly expectant expressions. The bottle of Blue Gall was sitting ominously on the counter again, but we did not take it seriously. Casey stepped forward with a piece of notebook paper in his hands as if he intended to read a list of our complaints, but we knew he wasn't going to read anything. Being a lawyer's son came in mighty handy sometimes. He cleared his throat and in a formal tone of voice stated,

"We, the Oppressed members of the C.I.T. Staff, have elected Toby to be our Spokesman, with the stated intention of *Airing Our Grievances.* Toby?"

Toby stepped forward with a solemn, thoughtful expression on his face. From where I was standing it was plain to see that his lips had a distinct orange tint, and there were Orange Crush stains on his t-shirt. He took the paper from Casey, held it up and said:

"We the Oppressed Members of the C.I.T *Staff* wish to say... well... that is... ummm, *we* the members of the C.I.T. *Corps* wish to bring to light several concerns that *we*, the Oppressed Members of the C.I.T. *Group*, feel are very..."

And then that glazed, faraway look came over him, and he hesitated for a long moment, taking in a big breath of air that he gulped down. We knew what was coming. The H.R.I. said impatiently,

"Well, *come on* Toby, get it out!"

Toby replied, almost apologetically,

"Well, you see, its kind of like *this*..."

And *out* it came, the Alphabet Burp, the whole entire alphabet in one unbelievably unattractive deep voiced gurgly stream like a giant bullfrog possessed by The Otherworld.

"*A, B, C, D, E, F, G, H, I, J, K, L, M, N, O, P, Q, R, S, T, U, V, W, X, Y, Z!*"

The H.R.I.'s face froze. The Flunkies faces froze, but when Toby got all the way to "Z", the H.R.I. aimed an accusing finger at him and shouted in a voice of judgement and doom,

"Get him! Blue Gall him! I *warned* you guys! Get him! *Get* them! Tackle all of them! Blue Gall *all* of them!"

At his command two of The Flunkies jumped forward grabbing at Toby, and the other two came for the rest of us. They weren't fooling around either. We all tried to bolt out of the Tack Room through its one narrow doorway with the Flunkies in hot pursuit. Four of us managed to escape, but Toby didn't make it. He had been collared by the other two Flunkies, and in spite of his struggles, they held him fast. The door to the Tack Room was slammed shut with a bang. We were on the outside, and Toby was trapped in there with The Flunkies and the H.R.I. in a state of high dudgeon. Then we remembered the bottle of Blue Gall that had been positioned ominously on the Tack Room counter. We realized that had been the H.R.I.'s plan all along. This was real trouble. We heard sounds of struggling and Toby resisting them, and then the door was flung open and he came flying out yelling,

"Run! Run! Blue Gall! Run!!"

And run we did. We ran right through the barnyard, right out the gate, and all the way up the road to the main cabin area. We ran right into Casey's cabin and all collapsed breathlessly on the floor. After a minute or two we caught our breath and all sat up. Casey stared at Toby, and pointed at his face, speechless. We all looked at him in turn and saw with a shock that the left side of Toby's face was a deep, dark, iridescent blue. They had Blue Galled him just as the H.R.I. had threatened to do, but he had struggled out of their grasp before they could get his entire face covered. He looked scarier than that Scots warrior guy in "Braveheart". We stared at him, shocked and silent. Toby stood up and went to look at himself in the cabin's mirror. He turned back to us with a strange, calm aura about him, and then with a wicked, dead serious expression on his blue and white face he declared,

"This... means... *War*. Those guys went too far this time. We need to make a solemn pact, all together, right here, right now, that we will get our *revenge* on them starting immediately, this evening at dinner... hands in the middle"!

He put his hand out palm down and looked at us with that same wicked expression on his half-blue face. We gathered around him and one by one placed our hands on top of his. He looked around at all of us and said,

"Ok, we're all in this together, Brothers In Arms! Down with Tyranny! Down with the H.R.I. and the Flunkies! Now, what should be our first act of Revenge?"

And, of course, it was *me* who spoke up first. In a hesitant voice, fully aware of the direction we were all heading towards with all of this, I began to outline a plan to launch our counter attack on the H.R.I. and the Flunkies. I was inspired by Toby's frog-like burping voice, and thought it would be a fitting revenge if I could manage to make it happen. The growl of approval that greeted my words gave me a warm glow of pure adolescent risk-taking joy. It was one for all and all for one, and we were united in our determination to fight back. We truly were Brothers In Arms. I said, very slowly and carefully,

"I think I have an idea... I am pretty sure it will work, but I'll need a jar with a secure top, and I'll need to get down to the lake right away and capture a medium sized frog."

Chapter 14

The Frog In The Soup

NOW PLEASE DON'T GET ME wrong, I love animals. I rescue earthworms that I find struggling helplessly on paved surfaces. I keep a bird feeder in my backyard full of sunflower seeds every winter, and I put out Hummingbird feeders every summer. I have rescued numerous turtles along major highways and country roads often at the risk of my own safety. I have a deeply rooted dislike of hunting and trapping, or anything that is unfair and cruel to animals. So please, *please* believe me when I say I am still *very, very, sorry,* for what happened to the frog, it was not my intention, honest. And may I add in my defense that I have been particularly nice to frogs ever since that time at camp, although I must say whenever I see a stainless steel soup tureen it still gives me the willies, the same way that a can of rubber cement still does. My plan for revenge was simple yet classically disruptive, but just as many other ideas of mine often went flying off the rails, this one did too, except this one *jumped* off the rails more than it flew.

Each evening at dinner all of the Campers and Counselors and C.I.T.s would gather at our assigned tables in the Dining Hall. Each table sat ten people, one at each end and four down each side. The Waiter sat at one end, and the Table Head sat at the other end. We rotated being the Waiter on a weekly basis. We C.I.T's sat at the H.R.I's table along with four of the Senior campers. The Waiter, me on this particular night, always arrived early to help set the table and make sure everything was in order. Each place setting had a soup bowl turned upside down on the plate. The soup was always served in a large stainless steel tureen with a cover and a ladle. The Table Head would remove the tureen's cover which was the signal for everyone to turn over their bowls. Then the Table Head would serve the soup. It was a foolproof system on most nights. I mean what could go wrong with serving soup?

As planned, I had run down to the lake with a pretty good sized jar I had secured and had captured a pretty good sized frog. For dinner that night I arrived extra early with my little froggy friend safe in the jar which was nestled in the front pocket of my camp sweatshirt. There was nothing unusual about me having my hands inside the front pocket of my sweatshirt. I went right to our table and immediately set the Table Head's bowl in its correct upside down position on the plate. After a quick look around to make sure I was not being observed by the kitchen staff, I unscrewed the jar, pulled out the frog, and snuck it under the upside down soup bowl. The bowls were the old fashioned, indestructible, heavy crockery kind, and they weighed a good bit. There was no chance a frog could push that bowl over and escape. I calmly set the rest of the bowls in place and went to the kitchen area to fetch our table's tureen of very, very, *steaming hot* soup. I think it was Chicken Noodle, but it really doesn't matter now.

All of the campers and staff filed in as usual and took their places around their respective tables. The H.R.I. took his seat at the head of our table. Carter, Casey, Gino, and Toby all sat on one side with Toby closest to my end, as far from the H.R.I. as he could get. He had vainly scrubbed his face for a long time and had managed to tone down the iridescence of the Blue Gall, but basically one half if his face was dark blue. He kept glaring at the H.R.I. with a look of pure venom that was elevated to a frighteningly alien level by the Blue Gall. There was an awkward silence at the table even though the H.R.I. made a few pathetic attempts at light banter.

All of the waiters went to the serving window and received our tureens of very, very *steaming hot* soup. Holding them carefully by the handles, we carried them to our tables, me being the first to do so. I set the tureen down in front of the H.R.I, maybe two feet from his place setting, and then went to my seat at the far end of the table. Just at that moment we all heard a strangely muffled "*Ribbit*!" coming from somewhere nearby. The H.R.I. looked around and asked,

"Was that a *frog*?"

Everyone looked around for the source of the sound, me included, and Casey suggested, in a very controlled tone,

"Umm... I think it was a cricket, maybe over there by the door over there? *Hear it*?"

Toby, Gino, Carter, and I nodded approvingly and made generalized sounds of agreement. We were very good actors when necessary. The H.R.I. gave us a piercing, suspicious look, and I had to look down at my plate because that was just too funny for me. A *cricket*? Yes, of course, maybe the World's Largest Cricket, like a cricket that had been the subject of some kind of genetic experiment gone bad. We struggled manfully to control our mirth. The H.R.I. stared at us suspiciously again. No one offered any further theories.

Regardless of the discovery of the World's Largest Cricket, the H.R.I. removed the cover of the soup tureen, and all of us turned our bowls over on our plates. Steam was rising off of the soup. It was very, very, *steaming* hot. I watched the H.R.I intently. This was going to be a good one, but I just didn't know how good it was really going to be. I found myself studying my soup spoon as if it were some kind of sacred artifact unearthed from an ancient burial mound.

The H.R.I. turned over his own bowl... and there was the frog sitting like a little green froggy statue on the H.R.I.'s plate, eyes open, throat faintly pulsing, but otherwise utterly motionless. It was awesome. It was incredible. It was better than I had imagined. The H.R.I.'s eyes widened with disbelief, his mouth opened, but no sound came out. At that exact same moment everyone at the table let out a shout of incredulous surprise and amazement mixed with the beginnings of hysterical laughter. The shouting startled the frog and shocked it into action. It reacted to the startling shouts by jumping in a high arc off of the H.R.I's plate straight towards my end of the table and splashing down right into the open tureen of very, very *steaming hot* soup. And I am very, very, *very* sorry to have to report that it died *instantly* upon plunging into the intensely hot soup. I mean *instantly*. Dead as a doornail. Stone cold dead, except it was more like hot soup dead. And there it was, right before our eyes, a pretty good sized frog, still in the full out jumping position, eyes wide open, floating in the soup, but really, *really* dead. The entire table went crazy like wild lunatics all gone totally nuts. Everyone was convulsed with shocked laughter over the pure horribleness of the moment. And then, just when the pandemonium had a possible chance of subsiding, the poor frog rolled completely over, belly up, stiff as a board, really, totally, *absolutely* dead.

Well, the entire camp, I mean like 100 people of all ages, stood up at their tables to see what the commotion was about. Many of the younger kids came rushing over to our table, and every single one of them went nuts too. It was a full blown civil disturbance of epic proportions. Kids were screaming with laughter, the Counselors weren't even trying to pretend it wasn't the most insane thing they had ever witnessed, and in the midst if it all sat the H.R.I., his mouth was still open, shocked into a statue-like pose not unlike the Frog's, the ladle still poised in his hand. It was beyond my wildest dreams.

The Camp Director rushed over too, and even he was having trouble keeping control of himself, but it wasn't even possible. Everyone was imitating the poor frog, holding their arms and hands out in front of them with their eyes staring and their mouths wide open, turning their upper bodies over slowly. It was total madness. It probably took a good ten minutes before everyone was finally settled back down at their tables, ours included. The offending tureen with the still floating very dead frog had been carried away by someone, and then, just as it looked like we might actually return to a semblance of normal human behavior, Casey asked, in a loud, whining and spoiled tone,

"*Does this mean we don't get any soup*?!!"

And that pretty much did it for the H.R.I. Instead of trying to repress the resulting hilarity and mayhem, he got up and stalked right out of the dining room in stony silence. We knew we had won that round, and we knew *he* knew we had been responsible for the Frog In The Soup. It didn't take a genius to figure out that things were going to get pretty rough for us from this point forward, but honestly, we didn't care. We were ready. We still had a few tricks up our sleeves like the Peanut Butter Shoes, and as a very last resort we still had the Fat Boy of summer camp pranks, we still had, The Thundering Herd.

Chapter 15

The Peanut Butter Shoes and The Thundering Herd

A S PRANKS GO, THE PEANUT Butter Shoes was such a no-brainer that it's hard to believe we didn't get tired of it, but it never failed to succeed, ever. I guess it proved that there are times when common, every day Boyish Dumbness still has a place in the world. The essentials of the prank were simple. When we went on overnight camping rides, the kitchen staff always provided us with several quart sized jars of peanut butter, huge jars of jam, and tons of good old fashioned Wonder Bread for our mid-day breaks. It would have been surprising if we had all failed to see those big jars of Skippy as the means to some kind of high jinks and shenanigans. We saw the possibilities, and very happily acted upon it.

At some point it had occurred to Carter that it would be hilariously weird to get up during the night and fill some poor victim's sneakers or shoes full of peanut butter. And I mean *full*, completely full, right up to the top edge of whatever footwear was chosen. The expression on his victim's face, upon attempting to push his foot into a solid mass of peanut butter at 6 o'clock in the morning was priceless. The raw stupidity of this prank just killed us.

Carter experimented with us first, because after all, what are close friends for? After being a victim of the Peanut Butter Shoes you either had to throw the shoes out or spend a lot of time diligently removing the peanut butter and then washing the remaining amount out. But in spite of those efforts, your socks and feet smelled like peanut butter for a very long time if you tried to wear those shoes or sneakers again. Carter did it to a pair of low-top Keds that I had, and I just threw them out. I felt it was the wisest choice.

In keeping with our sworn duty to wage war upon the H.R.I. and The Flunkies, Carter's ultimate goal was to fill a pair of the Head Riding Instructor's knee high rubber muck boots up to the ankles with Skippy Chunk Style, but he had never attempted it. We estimated it would take about two of the biggest jars of peanut butter to achieve this milestone. The real trick would be how to get a hold of the H.R.I's.'s boots, and since they would be more or less ruined in the process, it wasn't a realistic goal. However, now that the War was truly *on*, we were past the point of imposing limits on what was possible. The Frog In The Soup had set the bar pretty high, and Carter wanted to raise it higher.

We had one thing in our favor. The H.R.I disliked dirt and disorder, therefore he always left his rubber muck boots outside on the front steps of his cabin in order to keep any mud and manure from finding its way onto his cabin's floors. All we had to do was wait for everyone to fall asleep and then snatch the boots. Carter would diligently fill them with peanut butter, and then we would return them to their usual place before the morning Horsemen call. We all got up at 6 AM to bring in the horses, so our plan was to have at least one of us on hand to witness the consternation and hilarity we expected to ensue when the H.R.I. attempted to put his feet into boots packed with peanut butter.

But we had one thing that was *not* in our favor. It was called Clearing Patrol. This was a duty shared by all of the Counselors on a rotating basis. It required the Clearing Patrol counselor to stand watch in the middle of the Senior Clearing each night until midnight to keep an eye on things and make sure that everyone stayed in their cabins after Lights Out. We needed a distraction, a diversion, to hold the Clearing Patrol counselor's attention while we snatched the H.R.I.'s boots. In order to do this we resorted to one of the oldest pranks in the book, Streaking. Yes, good old fashioned Streaking. Running semi-naked or totally naked around the Clearing, but avoiding identification or capture by the Clearing Patroller. But in order for it to be a truly effective distraction, we collectively decided to bring out the Heavy Artillery, the Biggest Gun we had in our arsenal, our final ultimate weapon of mass summer camp hysteria, The Thundering Herd.

The Thundering Herd was Gino's invention. It took the classically disruptive idea of Streaking and elevated it to a higher level. The Herd, as we called it, involved a *minimum* of four Streakers who would run in a tight formation around the Clearing, shoulder to shoulder, all in step, but maintaining a complete and total silence. Five or six runners were better, and we had once achieved a total of eight which gave us two lines of four abreast, but four still did the trick. The effect upon an unsuspecting observer was impossible to describe accurately. I had volunteered to share a Clearing Patrol one night and had witnessed the Herd in action. It was a lot like my sighting of the The Scary Old Cowboy Guy And His Wild Horse. I ended up not wanting to admit I had seen it, and it was best not to mention it to anyone else since no one ever admitted to having seen it either.

As I recall it, there I was, sharing that night's Clearing Patrol with a Counselor friend who was pretty good on the banjo. He was quietly picking away on his banjo, and we were comfortably settled into big Adirondack chairs, taking in the night sky and the soft summer night air. Stars were twinkling overhead. We had a big Coleman Lantern that was hissing comfortingly, shedding its weird glow of white light. It was peaceful and serene. We had flashlights and a big canteen full of Bug Juice, our totally artificial basic camp beverage that came in assorted *colors* not flavors. It was about 11:30 PM and all was well, or so we thought.

Then off in the distance, just barely within our range of hearing, we caught a faint deep drumming sound, and I felt the ground begin to vibrate slightly beneath my feet. We heard heavy breathing coming closer and closer, but no voices. I waved my flashlight around trying to see what was approaching, and then the Herd appeared suddenly, materializing silently out of the darkness. They looked like nearly naked ghosts in the misty night running four abreast, in step, legs and feet pounding along, breathing in unison... and then they were gone again. The thudding of their bare feet receded into the blackness off the night. That was it, one fleeting glimpse in the misty glow of the Coleman Lantern, and that was all we saw. It was eerie, and unsettling, and weird.

Therefore, as a distraction, the Thundering Herd had no rival, and we resorted to it in order to get a shot at snagging the H.R.I's boots. Plus, we knew it would be another victory in our war against authority, But this night was not destined be the triumphant achievement that we had planned it to be. We, the

Herd, began our run at exactly 11:45 PM when we knew the Clearing Patroller would be ready to call it a night. It was me, Gino, Toby, and Casey. We set off from the lower end of the Clearing, all four of us having crept out of our own cabins at the agreed time. Carter was going to grab the boots when we had the full attention of the patroller, and then put the peanut butter in them and return them before our 6 AM wake up call.

We swept along the ground, running in step silently, intent upon our mission. We picked up the pace as we neared the Clearing Patroller's station. We could see the pool of white light created by the Coleman Lantern, just as we expected. We broke into the circle of light, maintaining our formation, but there, sitting in the two Adirondack chairs were not the Clearing Patrol Counselors we expected to see. To our utter and complete surprise we realized that the Clearing Patroller on this night was the Camp's Owner, Mr. Freeman, accompanied by his wife, Mrs. Freeman. They were the last two people on earth that we expected to see. Their faces were frozen, their mouths were locked shut, and they were totally immobilized. I mean, they never moved a muscle. The shock and surprise we experienced caused us to instantly break up our formation and scatter as fast as we could. All thoughts of the H.R.I.'s boots were gone from our minds.

I flew across the Clearing towards my cabin. I was the C.I.T in charge of three campers who were all asleep in their bunks. I slithered up the side of the cabin by my bunk, pulled myself up and over the window sill as quietly as I could and slipped into my sleeping bag in a few stealthy seconds. I lay there trying to control my breathing, hoping the campers wouldn't wake up. I was also hoping desperately that the other guys had made it back to their cabins without being identified. Then I heard voices out in the Clearing. I stole a glance over the edge of my window sill and saw flashlight beams sweeping back and forth in the darkness. I recognized Mr. Freeman's voice, and realized he was in conversation with the H.R.I. and two of the Flunkies who had been all roused out of their bunks. I heard the H.R.I. say to Mr. Freeman,

"It's those troublesome C.I.T.s sir, they're behind all of these pranks and disruptions. They're rebellious and disrespectful, and they have to be *punished*!"

Mr. Freeman replied sternly,

"Well then, I need proof! I want you to check all of the cabins and see who isn't in their bunks. Whoever isn't in their bunks will feel my wrath. You find them, and then I want those Streakers in my office immediately, tonight, and anyone who we catch out of their bunk is going to be on a bus for home first thing in the morning. If you can't do your job and control them, I will. So start searching, now!"

He sounded dead serious. He was going to send anyone that was a suspect in tonight's escapade straight back home. This threat made me feel very uncomfortable, and the whole idea was really scary. I continued watching as they began to go into each of the cabins, intent upon finding the culprits. When I saw the flashlight beams coming toward my cabin, I rolled over, pulled my sleeping bag over my head and did my absolute best imitation of The Innocently Sleeping Adolescent. The flashlight beam came cutting into the dark of my cabin, and I knew that the H.R.I and one of the Flunkies were standing in the doorway moving the flashlight beam from bunk to bunk. H.R.I. proclaimed loudly,

"Roll call! Wake up you guys... everyone here?"

I sat up holding my hand in front of my face as if to ward off the harsh beam of the flashlight. I kept blinking and looking confused, and saw my three campers all doing the same thing in their bunks. I was praying that the sweat I had wiped from my face was not visible. The flashlight beam swept my direction, and I threw my hand up against it again as if the light bothered my eyes. In a sleepy and bewildered voice I asked,

"What's going on? What time is it? What are you doing? Who are you looking for? It's *midnight*!!"

The H.R.I did not respond. He moved the flashlight around to each of the bunks and saw that everyone was accounted for. Without a word he turned, went out the door and down the steps, and moved on to the next cabin. I fell back onto my bunk and didn't move a muscle. The campers seemed to sense that something very serious was happening, and they stayed quiet too. I watched as the H.R.I. worked his way from cabin to cabin searching vainly for empty bunks, but our luck had held. Everyone had made it back in time. After a while the lights all went out again and silence fell on the Clearing.

At our 6 AM Horsemen Call the following morning, the hushed silence of the night was shattered by a loud commotion coming from the doorway of the H.R.I.'s cabin. In spite of our close call at midnight, Carter had completed his part of the job. During the confusion of the search for the Thundering Herd culprits, he had made good on his dream of perpetrating The Peanut Butter Shoes on the H.R.I.'s knee high rubber barn boots. The commotion was being made by the H.R.I. who had attempted to put on his boots and had stuck his foot right into three inches of Skippy Chunk Style. The confusion and consternation did not die down for a very long time, and believe me, we were meek as church mice for the entire day.

But this was the end of our night-time adventures. Mr. Freeman ordered big flood lights to be installed in a number of strategic places on the Clearing, and the Clearing Patrol became a real *patrol*. The Patrollers had to make the rounds every fifteen minutes and check each cabin to make sure everyone was where they should be. Our late night escapades were brought to a halt, but we had scored some big points in our battle with the H.R.I. Things completely subsided as the summer moved on, and an unofficial truce was observed willingly by us and cautiously by our adversaries. The close call of the Herd with Mr. Freeman and his wife was too close for comfort. None of us wanted to be sent away from camp, so we suspended hostilities and did our best to enjoy our days together and all the crazy-fun things that we still did on horseback. In fact, the more we channeled our rebellious energies into the mounted field games and our overnight camping rides into the surrounding countryside, the crazier it all got.

Chapter 16

The Horse That Wouldn't Stop

W HISKEY MAN BECAME A LIVING legend that summer. His unusual coloring, plow horse conformation, athleticism, and raw speed, set him apart from the other horses at camp. He had a kind and forgiving nature and was as docile as a lamb to work around, but it was plain as could be that he simply loved galloping at top speed with total disregard for his own safety. This fit perfectly with my own well established tendencies to ignore the basic rules of self preservation. Participation in the field games on Whiskey Man was a pure delight to me. We had an understanding between us that was all our own. We were always in the thick of it during Red Rover, Tag, or Cross The Delaware, and we didn't miss a Cavalry Charge. But of all the escapades that we shared, there were two that stood out the most memorable. One was a nearly fatal game of Cross The Delaware, and the other was a never-to-beforgotten downhill runaway episode that happened on a camping ride.

Cross The Delaware was a simple game. We would ride out into the huge fields that surrounded the camp and select one rider to be the first Guard. The Guard would take up a position in the middle of the field, and all of the other riders would make a line at the far end of the field facing their horses towards the Guard. At each end of the field was a designated Safe Zone. A rider couldn't be captured once he got into the Safe Zone. As soon as everything was organized and everyone's girths had been tightened, the Guard would call out,

"Cross the Delaware!"

At this signal, the riders at the far end of the field, usually thirty or more, would gallop their horses straight across the field towards the Guard with the goal of reaching the Safe Zone on the other side without being captured. Once captured a rider would join the Guard in the middle of the field and then help try to capture other riders in the next round. This would continue until only one horse and rider were left standing as the winner, and then that rider would become the Guard for the next round of the game. Capturing a rider could be accomplished in three different ways which all required a good bit of boldness, speed, and agility, not to mention reckless-ness.

Method 1. The Guard could ride up alongside of his intended captive, grab onto his shirt or his arm, and hold on long enough to shout out,

"One, Two, Three, I got you!"

Method 2. The Guard could ride up alongside of his intended captive, *pretend* to grab his arm or shirt, but then swiftly lean down, get his hand behind the rider's boot and flip his leg up, propelling the rider out of the saddle. Yes, we would actually try to flip our opponent right out of the saddle. Like I said earlier, you could never play these games today.

Method 3. The Guard could ride up alongside of his intended captive, but instead of trying to grab him or flip him out of the saddle, he would reach out, get his fingers under the crown piece of the horse's bridle and deftly slip it over the horse's ears. This tactic caused the bit to drop right out of the horse's mouth as the bridle fell to the ground, which in turn caused the horse to come to a complete stop.

All of the camp's horse's were trained to come to a full stop if their rider fell off, or if the bridle broke, or became undone or unbuckled for some reason. Regardless of which method a Guard chose to try, it required agility, courage, and a bold attitude to win these brief one-on-one encounters while galloping along side by side with another horse. It also required that the Guard have a horse that liked to run, had acceleration, and didn't mind a bit of physical

contact. Whiskey Man had all of the above require-
ments, and I loved the exhilarating, mock battle feel
of the game. As I mentioned before, the rules stated
that the last rider captured became the Guard for the
next round of the game.

Whiskey Man and I were rarely captured that
summer. The horse could not be caught once he had
a lead, and he had the coordination and instincts of a
cutting horse which is most likely what he had been
before being shipped East. So we were always one of
the last horses and riders not captured, having
managed to outrun or outmaneuver all of the other
horses. As I became increasingly confident in
Whiskey Man's ability to accelerate and escape from
any pursuers, I got in the habit of taunting them a
little bit just for fun. Usually this was accepted as
harmless fun, but on this particular day my arrogance
got under Carter's skin. It turned out that he really
did not like to see me win nearly every time. I kind of
knew that, so it was bad sportsmanship on my part,
and not too smart either.

On the day in question, we were playing Cross
The Delaware in a big field that had a stone wall at
its far end, crowned with barbed wire fencing to keep
cattle from going over the wall in search of greener
pastures. The field had been planted to corn the year
before, but it had been plowed and harrowed recently
and was lying fallow for this season. It was uneven in
places but really huge, just right for the game.

Carter was riding The Gray Goose that day. Goose was a thoroughbred who was no slouch, but he wasn't a sprinter as much as he was a jumper. Carter had a determined look on his face and came charging after us with all-out commitment. I cantered Whiskey Man across the mid-line of the field and then confidently loitered there, just daring Carter to try and capture me. I waited until he was fairly close, then turned Whiskey Man's head toward the Safe Zone and let him loose. He dug in those big hind feet of his, accelerated in his unusual breathtaking style and began to pull away. I couldn't resist turning around in the saddle and smirking at Carter as we galloped off. This made him mad, and he continued to pursue us. I kept turning around to make faces at him, and in so doing I failed to see that while we were not in danger of being caught from behind, we were rapidly running out of real estate up ahead.

I turned forwards in the saddle again and realized we were only a few strides away from the end of the field and its stone wall topped with the strands of barbed wire. I hauled hard on the left rein, and Whiskey Man made a valiant attempt to turn away from the wall, but just when it looked like we were going to make it, his feet went right out from under him on the soft ground. He went straight down onto his right side while we were still moving at top speed and slammed into the earth as if a rug had been pulled out from beneath him. The impact was heavy, and it all happened in the blink of an eye.

In spite of how sudden and violent the crash was, when we plowed into the ground, everything shifted into slow motion exactly like everyone always says it does in life-threatening situations. My many experiences of falling off of moving horses stood me in good stead that day as my instinctive natural reactions took over. I instantly pulled both of my feet out of the stirrups and more or less executed a flying dismount just as Whiskey Man's right side slammed into the ground. If my right foot had still been in the stirrup, I am quite sure my right leg would have been badly mangled or crushed against the ground by Whiskey Man's body.

The reins were still in my left hand, and as we went down I instinctively reached out to break the fall with my right hand and forearm. It's amazing how hard the impact was against the softly tilled soil. For a few, seemingly endless, slow motion moments Whiskey Man and I slid along the freshly harrowed furrows side by side, and came to a sudden stunned stop in the churned up earth. But before we stopped, while we were still sliding, everything was crystal clear to me. It was as if I were watching a movie of a horse and rider crashing to the ground in super slow motion from somewhere above me but simultaneously from my own point of view as we slid along the ground together.

Whiskey Man's broad back and the saddle I had just vacated were only inches away from my face. The stirrups were bouncing around crazily at the ends of the stirrup leathers, and good sized stones were popping up into the air along with clods of turf and clouds of dusty dirt. His entire body was undulating over the surface of the ground, and I remember seeing his feet and legs thrashing forward and back as if he were still trying to run. And then, in the next instant, we had come to a grinding stop and just lay there side by side. We were covered in dirt and clouds of dust we had kicked up were hovering in the air and settling all around us.

I still had the reins gripped in my left hand, but my right arm and right leg did not feel too good. I began to move my legs and arms gingerly and determined I was still in one piece. I sat up. Whiskey Man rolled into an upright position and began to struggle to his feet, so I stood up too. The right side of my body from my shoulder to the toe of my badly scraped right boot was covered in dirt. I had dirt down the inside of that boot too. I had a couple of pretty impressive abrasions on my right arm and my rib cage, and my t-shirt was torn. I had dirt all over my face and in my hair, but other than that I was mostly just stunned from the fall.

Whiskey Man was a real mess. He looked like he had scraped the right side of his body against a giant piece of dirt covered sand paper. There was dirt all over his face and neck, all along his ribcage, and on his hindquarters and right hind leg. The right hand side of the saddle was destroyed, and the right hand side stirrup leather had been torn off. On his right shoulder he had deep gouges filled with dirt, and a big flap of skin hanging down. The blood from these cuts and gouges was mixed with the dirt clinging to him, and he just looked awful.

As I began to assess the damage, the other guys came galloping up led by Carter. They dismounted and began talking and carrying on all at the same time. From their point of view the crash had been spectacularly violent. No one could believe I hadn't broken anything, and that I was more or less ok. Poor Whiskey Man had taken the brunt of the crash, and all we could do was lead him back to camp, slowly and painfully, while a couple of the guys rode ahead to get some medical help. I refused to leave him and limped along next to him patting his neck on the undamaged side and murmuring encouragement to him. As we hobbled along towards the stables he turned and rubbed his dirt covered head against my shoulder every few steps. Our bond was closer now than ever.

In spite of the shocking damage to his right shoulder, once we were able to hose him off and clean him up a bit, he had come through the crash in reasonably good shape. A bucket of water and an extra ration of sweet feed perked him up as well.

Eventually, the Vet came and stitched the flap of skin back into place on his shoulder and put bandages here and there. We applied Red Gall and Blue Gall in a variety of places too. He endured all of this discomfort stoically, not even making a fuss when the sutures went in. He ended up getting about twenty stitches in his poor shoulder, and was stiff and sore for a week or so. He looked bizarre with the multiple splotches of Blue Gall and Red Gall all over his bruised and scraped right side. Against his natural pink and grey coloring those red and blue splotches made him look like a Jackson Pollock painting.

Given the violence and severity of our crash, the general consensus was that we had both gotten off easy. I retold the story of the crash many times. I made sure everyone knew how Whiskey Man had tried to save both of us from my arrogant lack of awareness. I described how he had tried to make that desperate left hand turn even before I had hauled on the reins, but that the recently tilled ground had betrayed him. I was grateful to him for saving me more than I could adequately express, and tended to him and cared for him like a baby during his recovery. Who knows what would have happened if we had hit the stone wall with the barbed wire fence at the top. It was best not to think about it.

Inactivity was not one of Whiskey Man's strong points so a week of stall rest and hand walking may have been good for his shoulder, but it wasn't good for his mind. After a week I was allowed to tack him up and take him around the riding ring at a walk. After a second week of light work we joined in on what was supposed to be a quiet overnight ride to one of our nearby camping sites. It was a Horseman Only Overnight. Everyone else was able to just enjoy the ride, chase each other all over the place on their horses, and not be stuck having to babysit any of the regular campers. Whiskey Man was under strict orders to walk and trot, and I was determined to stick to those limitations, but it was frustrating for him to see all the activity and not be included. I felt like I was sitting on one of those Brahma Bulls at the Rodeo, just waiting for the chute to open.

I made a point of staying with the Slow Group, walking along at the back of the pack content to enjoy the beautiful day out on the country roads riding my all-time favorite horse. Unfortunately, Whiskey Man was not in the same relaxed frame of mind as I was. As we walked along the road he began to break into short little choppy trotting steps, shifting his hind-quarters from side to side against the restriction of the bit and reins. I kept him under control for a while, but after about half an hour of this he was really pulling against me so I let him move to the front of the Slow Group which seemed to calm him down, or so I thought.

The Fast Group was about a quarter of a mile ahead of us hidden from our view by a rise in the road. As we came over the top of the rise they came back into view, and Whiskey Man's ears perked forward. He began pulling hard against the reins, breaking into that short choppy trot, and swinging his hindquarters from side to side again. The horses behind us picked up on his frustration, and they started to trot too. In a few minutes the whole Slow Group was gathered around us, trotting together, and this caused him to increase his pace. The other horses picked up their trot tempo in response. Even though I was holding his reins as short as I could with his neck bowed against the bit, he managed to move into a slow agitated canter. The closer we got to the Fast Group, the more agitated and restless he became, and my arms were getting tired.

Now let's remember that Whiskey Man ran away with the Head Riding Instructor even though the H.R.I. was a fully grown adult, and a big strong guy too. I weighed about 140 pounds and was considered strong, but I was no match for the horse's one thousand pounds of agitated muscular energy. The slow restless canter began to become a forward flowing slightly faster canter, and I made the mistake of coming up out of the saddle in the jockey position to get a shorter grip on the reins. That was like flipping a switch to "On" in Whiskey Man's brain. He snapped his head forward snatching more rein from me and began to accelerate. The rest of the Slow Group increased their pace, but he and I pulled away from them again. Whiskey Man's sights were set on the Fast Group, and I was quickly losing my hold on him. I yelled ahead to warn the Fast Group,

"*Look out! Look out! I can't stop him! Look out!*"

We were coming up on them very quickly, but they had heard his hooves clipping against the hard dirt road and had already seen what was happening. A few of them pulled off to the side of the road to let us pass, but several of them made the bad decision of breaking into a canter in a vain attempt to stay ahead of us, and that was the final straw for Whiskey Man. Our relaxed ride through the countryside had disintegrated into a Country Fair style road race involving about a dozen horses. I was now a passenger on a horse that felt like a runaway freight train, but in my heart and soul I was loving every minute of it, and then some.

We were rapidly catching up to the Fast Group's horses that had tried to canter ahead of us, and I was not in control of Whiskey Man. Just when it looked like we were going to slam into the one of them, Whiskey Man swerved to the right like an NFL Halfback and leaped over the ditch that ran along the right hand side of the road. This section of the road was deeply sunken from untold years of wagons and tractors traveling on it, and it had steep grassy embankments on both sides. Whiskey Man landed on the face of the embankment and took three huge strides right along it above the ditch, his body leaning at a sharp angle, his left side being nearly parallel to the road surface. His powerful momentum carried him forward, and then he leapt back onto the road in front of the Fast Group's leading horses.

This small group included the H.R.I. and one of the best riders out of all the Horseman named Ryan who rode his own very fancy show jumping pony named Little Alfie. Little Alfie had a dark, golden honey colored coat beautifully offset with a blond mane and tail. He was fancy, fast, and he could jump higher than most of the full sized horses at camp. As Whiskey Man leaped horizontally off of the embankment, across the ditch again, and back onto the road, we landed a length or two ahead of Ryan and Little Alfie. In response, Ryan and Alfie put on a burst of speed. With me and Whiskey Man charging ahead in the lead, and with only Ryan and Little Alfie keeping pace right behind us, we left the Fast Group literally in the dust.

I had barely managed to stay in the saddle during Whiskey Man's three huge jaw dropping horizontal strides along the face of the embankment. As we landed securely back on the road surface, I settled myself into the saddle and took a strong hold on the reins, but there was no slowing him down now. He powered forward sending a shower of rocks and sparks flying out from beneath his hooves. I realized in a sudden flash that we were almost like The Scary Old Cowboy Guy And His Wild Horse. A quick look back at the faces of the rapidly diminishing Fast Group confirmed my realization. I knew that, in fact, we weren't *almost* like The Scary Old Cowboy Guy On His Wild Horse, we were *exactly* like them in so many ways. I was riding my own Wild Horse into the Sun, and I felt truly fulfilled.

But those were the only thoughts I had time for before we flew headlong along the gravelly dirt road as it pitched sharply downhill into a series of long curves. From a bird's eye view the road would have looked like a gigantic **S** about a mile long. This part of the road was mostly in shadow as we galloped through the steep embankments along both sides. We flew past driveways and mailboxes every few hundred feet. Farmhouses and barns were perched above the road on either side, but there were no people to be seen.

Suddenly, I heard wild laughter amidst the clattering of hooves.

I stole a quick look backwards and saw that Ryan and Little Alfie were still with us, galloping stride for stride. Ryan had an expression of pure joy on his face, and he was laughing uncontrollably. It was exhilarating and contagious, and I began laughing too. Time seemed to stand still for the next several minutes or so as we flew down those long looping curves. The two horses were running neck and neck. We had no hope of slowing them down, and it was like being in my own version of Heaven. Although, I distinctly remember looking down at my right boot in its stirrup and seeing the gravelly road streaming backwards beneath us like a huge conveyor belt, and thinking,

"If I fall off anywhere along here, it's really going to be bad."

As we came out of the final downhill right hand curve, with the sharply sloping grass embankments rising up along both sides, something happened that I will never forget. An older man, a farmer, in faded blue overalls and a white t-shirt, with a straw hat on his head, was trimming the weeds around the base of a mailbox with a pair of big old fashioned hand clippers. I remember that he had a pipe in his mouth too, and I caught a whiff of pipe tobacco smoke as we thundered past him. We went careening down that curving gravelly road and passed within maybe five feet of that old farmer guy trimming the weeds around his mailbox. The two horses were breathing like freight trains, rocks were skipping out from beneath their hooves, Ryan and I were laughing like lunatics, but that old guy *never even looked up*. Honest. It was as if the sights and sounds of two kids flying past him on out of control horses on an otherwise lazy summer afternoon was something he encountered every day, and he simply found it a total bore.

And then we swept out onto a level section of the road in the full glaring sunlight with open fields on either side. There were no ditches, embankments, or fences along it. I turned Whiskey Man's head into the field on our left, and Ryan did the same on Little Alfie. The field sloped up towards some trees a few hundred feet away, and I aimed towards them. Whiskey Man saw the trees and finally, thankfully, began to slow down. Ryan had turned Alfie towards the trees too, and in unison we slowly came down to a slow canter and then, mercifully, down to a trot. Whiskey Man made one more turn away from the trees, and finally the two horses came down to a walk. Ryan and I looked at each other and just started laughing again. We dismounted and walked the horses back toward the road, cooling them off and resting ourselves a bit too. Eventually we made our way back to the road and waited for the rest of the group to catch up.

To be perfectly honest I have no memory of the rest of that day's ride, but that mad dash down the big **S** curves of that hard dirt road was engraved into my brain forever. That flat-out gallop on Whiskey Man, side by side with Ryan and Little Alfie, flying down that road was the greatest moment of my life up to that point, and it made a permanent impression on me. I have relived it a million times, every detail sharp and clear. I have often wondered if that old farmer guy clipping the weeds around his mailbox had simply ignored us, or did we go thundering by so fast that he didn't even have time to react? I'll never really know the answer to that one, but I had fulfilled my dream without intending to, and it had been beautiful.

"Whatever else you leave Undone, just once, ride a Wild Horse into the Sun."

Contrary to my other crazy escapades, I *highly* recommend it.

Chapter 17

How To Have A Horse Almost Step On Your Head

T HE BIG FINALE OF THE camp season was Parents Weekend, the last weekend of the summer session. All of the campers participated in one way or another. Some of the kids exhibited displays of Arts and Crafts, and good number of campers had roles in the Camp Musical. There was a big Swimming Competition down at the lake, and then there was the grand finale, The Parents Weekend Horse Show. The camp brought in three judges to officiate the show and hired a professional announcer. We spent several days sprucing up the Riding Rings, painting up Show Jumps, and putting numbers and flags on the Cross Country Course. Then we spent an entire day grooming all the horses and braiding their manes and tails. It was exciting and fun, and it brought everyone together for a common purpose.

We, the C.I.T.s, had our own classes to compete in at the Parents Weekend horse show. We were judged riding on the Flat, over the Show Jumps, and on the Cross Country Course. Whiskey Man was not made for flatwork, and he was an inexperienced jumper, but on the Cross Country Course he did fairly well except that he always wanted to gallop too fast. I never knew if he was going to actually jump over the cross country obstacles or just smash right through them. I fell off pretty often out there, but the ground was soft, and he usually came to a complete stop while I dusted myself off and remounted. He always seemed a little apologetic afterwards and would behave for the next few jumps.

The centerpiece of the Cross Country course was the spanking new Drop Jump which we had built earlier that summer out of the railroad ties Constable Tom had insisted we "bring back to camp." When the C.I.T.s were ready to ride on the Cross Country course, all of the parents and campers gathered in the central viewing area so they could watch each of us negotiate the circuit of obstacles. There were eight jumps set out in a big circle with the Drop Jump being the second to last on the course. There were two Coops, two simple Logs, a Stone Wall, a Giant's Bench, an Up-Step, and the Drop Jump. There at least one hundred campers and parents on hand watching us that day with my parents among them. The moms and dads were dressed nicely, with skirts and high heeled shoes being the norm for the moms, and khakis and well polished Oxford shoes for the dads.

When my turn came, I concentrated on keeping Whiskey Man under control so he could approach the obstacles in good form. We cantered slowly up to the jumps, and he felt relaxed and comfortable as we went around. He managed first six jumps really well, and with the last two to go I was feeling confident. I had kept him on a short rein up to that point, but as we started up towards the Drop Jump he began to pull pretty hard as usual. The Drop Jump was purposefully located at the top of a small knoll to help keep the horses from gaining too much speed as they approached it. It was essentially a three sided rectangular excavation about five feet deep and eight feet wide, positioned on the downhill side of the knoll. The end where we jumped in and the two long sides were lined with tiers of railroad ties that we had spiked together. It was like a big three sided wooden box set into the ground, with the fourth side being the open end that we galloped out of on the way to the final obstacle on the course.

I steered Whiskey Man up the knoll still trying to maintain a slow canter. He was fighting with me, shaking his head from side to side trying to snatch more rein. We came up over the top of the knoll to the edge of the Drop Jump, and it took him completely by surprise. He put on the brakes and slid to a halt with all four feet bunched together right at the edge of the top railroad tie. I was caught off guard by his sudden stop and fell forward with my arms around his neck, holding on for dear life as he teetered over the edge of the drop. He ducked his head to maintain his balance. I lost my hold and tumbled right over his head into the bottom of the Drop Jump. I landed in the sandy footing, rolled over onto my back and looked up to see Whiskey Man teetering above me. He was wobbling back and forth at the very edge of the drop, and it didn't look good. His weight was tipped forward, and it was obvious that he was not going to be able to recover his balance. I started to roll over to scramble out of there, but before I could, his front feet slipped over the edge, and he jumped in right on top of me. It looked like my luck had finally run out.

But just before he jumped, while he was still fighting for his balance, wobbling precariously on the edge, he turned his head and looked down at me. His right eye met my frightened gaze for one breathless instant, and then he jumped in. I scrunched my eyes shut and made an expectantly painful facial expression. It was exactly like when the dart was coming down from the ceiling just before it stuck in my head. I honestly felt like my life was coming to an end. There simply wasn't room for Whiskey Man to jump into that relatively small space and not trample all over me. It was a terrible feeling.

In the next moment he landed on the bottom of the Drop Jump, and everything became jumbled and confusing. There were multiple clattering sounds mixed with tromping and clomping noises as his big steel shod feet hit the ground all around me. Some of the sandy dirt splattered onto my riding jacket, and I felt my riding cap go flying off my head. One of his hooves had brushed by so closely that it had knocked my hard hat off and scraped my ear. And then everything went silent again, the noise and confusion was over. I kept my eyes scrunched up, and I remember wondering if I was dead, and then thinking,

"If someone is actually dead, can they still wonder about whether or not they are?"

I opened my eyes and realized that by some incredible miracle I was still lying in the same position at the bottom of the Drop Jump basically unharmed except for a scrape on my left ear. Whiskey Man's hoof prints were plain to see all around me and they were frighteningly close. I felt like one of those circus performers who serve as human targets and have those special knives thrown into the spaces all around them. But I knew that it hadn't really been a miracle. I knew that Whiskey Man had saved me yet again. In that breathless moment, when he had turned his head and looked me in the eye, he had sized up the situation, judging where to place his feet, and he had purposefully avoided stepping all over me. He had jumped in and landed with his big steel shod feet all around me, but had not even touched me except for knocking my hard hat off on his way out. It was a testament to his athleticism and coordination, and I was grateful beyond words.

The instant that I realized I was ok, I scrambled to my feet and climbed up out of the Drop Jump on the same side we had jumped in from. As I pulled myself up and looked over the edge of the top railroad tie all I remember seeing were hundreds of feet running towards me. A couple of hundred high heeled shoes, Oxford shoes, and swinging handbags were converging on the Drop Jump on the double. Every mom and dad at the horse show was running like mad towards the Drop Jump. It was a crazy sight to see. I climbed the rest of the way out and waved my hands to signal that I was ok, and about half a minute later I was engulfed by anxious adults who couldn't believe I hadn't been trampled to death. They all started brushing the dirt off of my jacket and fussing over me at once.

Their collective panic was very understandable. From their point of view up in the observation area it had been a scary sequence to watch. All they had seen was Whiskey Man come to a sliding stop at the edge of the Drop Jump and me tumble over his head and disappear into it. Then they saw him jump in after me and canter out of the Drop Jump alone, no sign of me. My mom told me later that my dad had sprinted towards the Dining Hall for the nearest telephone in order to call an ambulance because it looked like there was no chance I could have survived the incident without serious injury, or worse.

You might say my luck had stayed with me like in the early days of my misguided youth and its attendant risk taking, but I've always felt that there was a deeper and more important force at work. I've always believed that the real saving grace had been my soul to soul connection with Whiskey Man. I had connected with him and had saved him from being sent away from camp and back to the dealer. He had connected with me on that rare inner wavelength that some horses and lucky humans share, and then he had avoided trampling on me when I was lying on the bottom of the Drop Jump. In a strange and ironic twist he had saved my life just like I had saved the life of the Girl In The Pool. I had stood at the edge of the pool looking down into the water where the little girl lay helplessly. Whiskey Man had stood at the edge of the Drop Jump looking down to where I lay helplessly. I had saved the girl. He had saved me. Sometimes I find myself believing that good deeds really are rewarded after all.

Chapter 18

So Anyway, There I Was

S O THAT SEASON OF RIDING Camp came to an end, and I went home with a different outlook on life and a strange new sense of energy in my heart and mind. After spending my entire childhood dreaming about Knights, and Vikings, and exciting adventures, I had actually and truly ridden my Wild Horse into the Sun. I had won my spurs, so to speak, and I knew I would always stay connected to that moment. My need for Risk had finally led to a Reward.

Something big happened to me that summer. I had learned to love life and to embrace its elemental qualities. My life had become grounded in the pure joy of galloping down a sunlit open country road in complete harmony with my horse, and in the company of my best friends. I had pierced through the layers of conventional experience and had discovered the most essential parts of who I was and what had meaning to me. It would prove to be the foundation of how I would live for the rest of my life.

So, anyway, there I was, two weeks away from starting 9th Grade at our town's High School. New friends and new experiences were awaiting me. New possibilities would present themselves. Beyond high school lay College lurking in the shadowy future. The Vietnam War was gathering its tragic strength. Rock and Roll had taken over the world, and Woodstock was only a summer away. But I had learned a simple and significant truth that would sustain me through the challenging years ahead... Once you ride a Wild Horse into the Sun, you can never go back, you can only go forward, galloping straight on towards the horizon, doing your best not to fall off. And you can't do that slowly or cautiously, because if you do, you'll miss out on most of the fun, and that really doesn't sound like much fun at all, does it?

Made in the USA
Lexington, KY
23 April 2014